When Platinum Rusts

V1

Outside the Script

Anka B. Troitsky

WHEN PLATINUM RUSTS

WHEN PLATINUM RUSTS

Copyright © 2025 Anka B. Troitsky

Published in the UK by Greystone
Consultancy LTD

ISBN: 978-1-0683590-1-9

To my first readers and true friends.

I'm grateful to my editor, Andrew Hodges, for your insight, patience, and care in shaping this book.

Contents

Epigraphica
Offering to the Temple of O'Teka RB-58946278

"I never met the woman. Not in the flesh.
I first heard her name from my father, the way men speak of a storm they survived.
By the time I stood near her — if I ever truly did — she was over ninety. I had no idea what ninety looked like on a legend. I did not know she was one.
Earth is gone. She is one of the reasons we are not.
Only her bones reached the colony.
They called her Selest the Cruel.
Maker of the Loaders.
The woman who reached into conception itself and tampered with the oldest human right — the right to choose what we become.
I once believed she was a monster who received her due.
But the deeper I looked, the less simple it became.
What terrified me was not what she did.
It was what she willingly paid for it.
If a mind as rigorously moral as Doctor Dvali's could cross that threshold — deliberately, eyes open — then what might any of us do, cornered by extinction?
Would we surrender our conscience and live on in unending pain to preserve the species?
Or would we perish clean beside it, and call that virtue?

— Rodion Baker, *Summary of the Earth Evacuation*, Second Edition (AC1011)

1: Dominic Veir

"Selest Dvali, marry me."

Aldo kneeled, perfectly composed, his smile so confident and unwavering. No trace of nerves. He knew what he was doing.

Selest, however, hadn't yet decided how to react. She had always known this day would come – she even knew now why it was today and not the day before or tomorrow.

They had come up to the top level of Two Tree Market for a new air purifier when they passed a boutique displaying wedding dresses.

Half-joking, Aldo suggested they step inside to *check out the latest fashion*. She hadn't thought much of it. But now here he was, kneeling in the changing room as if this had been his plan all along.

Selest didn't like traps.

"Why are you doing this to me?" she asked. "Couldn't you wait until the evening? The shortlist of winners won't arrive before noon."

Aldo's answer was exactly what she expected.

"I don't want to wait, Lesty, my love. I want to be with you forever. I finally decided."

"I want us to be together too," Selest replied cautiously, "but I'll have decisions to make when I get my result."

Aldo rose from his knee and now looked down at her, his eyes suddenly cold and searching. "So, if you're not on the list, you'll say yes, and if you are . . ."

He left the question hanging in the air.

"And if I am ... I don't know." Selest sighed. "Aldo, my entire future depends on this."

"And on your answer to my proposal too. We've been together for almost four years. We were happy. We planned to work together in a colony on Mars. You wanted children so much, and now ... this damned contest. Why did you even have to take part in it?"

Selest blinked in surprise at the tone in his voice. Annoyance, bitterness and a flash of anger she had never heard from him before. Her first impulse was to justify herself. "Darling, don't be angry. Don't frown so much. I didn't expect an opportunity to work for KOSI to open up. To miss such a chance ... Wait. What do you mean, 'too'? Would you leave me if I don't answer you here and now?"

Aldo closed his eyes, then smoothed the tension on his forehead. "I don't know either.

Jupiter's farther than Mars. With your surgical skills, you could build a great career in the cave town. At KOSI, though, you'd be starting over – as a trainee."

"But Aldo, we discussed plan B and even D. You're resourceful. You have more than one qualification. You could apply, too, and there's an additional chance if your spouse is already working at the station."

Aldo opened his eyes, and this time they flared with rage. "An application for what? For technical staff? To service heating systems instead of building a cave city under the red stone? And with a scientist wife too?"

Selest's anger flared in return. "I can't believe my ears. You told me you didn't care about such things. Have you been lying to me?"

It was as though a quarrel had stormed into the room, kicking the door open. But before it could take root, Aldo spun on his heel and left.

Selest stood alone in the elegant fitting room of the expensive boutique where Aldo had brought her to try on a wedding dress. It had been meant as a surprise, but it devolved into heartbreak.

Selest turned to the mirror. Minutes ago she had looked like a princess in the white frock with its five-metre crimson silk train, designed to flutter beautifully in the wind when they would emerge on the wedding balcony of the Great Elm. Now that vision seemed impossibly distant. Her raven-black curls still shimmered under the bright lights, but her brown eyes glistened with tears instead of joy.

"May I come in?" a soft voice asked.

"Of course," Selest replied, hastily wiping her eyes. It was the avatar of the shop assistant, Juniper, programmed to have an eternally enthusiastic expression.

"Madam, you look stunning in this one," Juniper gushed, her ghostlike face appearing in the corner of the mirror. "But I recommend requesting it a quarter size smaller."

"Thank you, but I won't be ordering this lovely dress," Selest said, her voice soaked with sadness.

"Too bad. Would you like to try another style? I recommend Cherry-Blossom-8, which would go wonderfully with your hair and—"

"I don't want to. Leave me, Juniper. Please."

The avatar murmured a polite farewell and vanished. Selest changed out of the dress and left the boutique. Only now did she notice the ring Aldo had slipped onto her finger during his proposal. A beautiful platinum band with a drop of ruby on it. Selest took it off and put it in her pocket. She would decide later what to do with it.

Aldo was nowhere to be seen. She didn't bother searching for him in other shops but went straight to the trunk-elevator and down to the underground garage. Once in her car, she decided not to go home yet. There was less than an hour until noon. She could pass the time studying or reading something in the Georgian language on her terminal. Perhaps she could even roll down the window, as the garage filters kept the sand and dusty winds outside.

The terminal's beep startled her. Her heart sank as she opened the message. The first word was not *Congratulations* but *Project KOSI would like to thank Selest Dvali for applying . . .*

She didn't read any further.

Two dreams shattered in a single day. Now she had neither a fiancé nor the promising career she had fantasised about for a year. She started the ZP engine and drove slowly to the exit. After passing through the first gate, she waited for it to close before the next one opened. In that half minute, a terrible thought struck her: she might not go to Mars either. Without Aldo, there would be no home, children or joy from the job in the surgical wing.

But it was not a broken woman who drove out into the dusty street. Determined and resolute, Selest was ready to shape a new future for herself. She wasn't a failure. She had a few qualifications, too, and a reasonably sharp mind.

The sky turned to rust as Selest drove through the last of the city's outskirts, her visor dimming against the red sunlight bleeding through the thick, dirty clouds. A low dust storm was building again, scouring the abandoned road margins and lifting fine grit against the windows of her sealed vehicle. She passed other cars – armoured, domed or patched with foil – most driven by people in long robes and breathing masks, their eyes hidden beneath dark hoods. Some walked instead, heads bowed against the wind, plastic sheeting wrapped tightly around their limbs.

Selest's route took her past glassy towers with internal gardens suspended like lanterns – green sanctuaries hanging mid-air – and low arcades where street markets had taken root under reinforced canopies. Inside, vendors traded hydroponic roots, canned fish and engineered fruit – safe from the air outside, thick with particles of a crumbling world. So different from the blue sky and clean air of the establishments at the top of the giant tree she just descended from.

Selest tightened her grip on the wheel. Every time she returned, the city looked a little more like something she might have built in a fever dream – functional, resilient and sealed off from the weather. And it had to be. With the sun changing and Earth left with perhaps a century of habitable time, survival no longer meant thriving. It meant containment.

With very few vehicles braving the desolate roads, Selest followed the faint glow of street lights that guided her through the winter streets shrouded in a swirling storm. After arriving safely at her block, she stepped into the familiar lobby of her building, her stride purposeful and unwavering, a silhouette of determination against the haze of an unforgiving season. She smiled at this analogy.

Inside the lobby, also designed like a small indoor market square, the grocery stalls were shuttered for their afternoon break, their vibrant awnings folded neatly away, leaving only the faint mingling scents of aromatic oils and perfumed goods drifting through the air. Meanwhile, the coffee shops bustled with activity as staff swiftly transitioned to restaurant mode, replacing sugar bowls with salt and pepper shakers, swapping tablecloths and preparing for the lunchtime crowd with practised efficiency.

Selest's hunger, suppressed by stress, now roared to life. She headed straight for her favourite place, *Aunt Tessie's*. The woman behind the counter waved at Selest, her warm smile and face glistening like a chocolate glaze.

"Today I've got your favourite Kyiv meatballs. What sauce will you have, Selest?"

"Tkemali, please," Selest replied, "and lots of fried onions. Thank you, Tessie."

Tessie leaned her great bosom conspiratorially over the counter. "Hey, look over there," she said, nodding at one of the tables.

Selest turned, her heart skipping. But it wasn't Aldo. A man in an expensive jumpsuit sat at the table, enjoying a bowl of soup.

"Who is he?" Selest whispered.

"No idea. But he's been waiting for you for an hour," Tessie replied, setting Selest's usual order on the tray. "Had to feed him."

"What does he want?"

"Didn't ask. Here, have some extra mash. For free."

"Thank you. Hmmm ... Well, let him finish eating," Selest said, winking at Tessie before taking her tray towards a table far from the stranger.

The man's meal didn't take much longer. After scooping the last drops, he wiped his mouth with a cloth napkin and approached Selest's table with well-measured and deliberate movements. She looked up as his shadow loomed over her.

"Ms Dvali, may I have a word?" he asked, his voice low and formal.

Selest gestured to the empty chair opposite her, spearing a meatball with her fork and dipping it into the sauce. "Go for it."

The man sat down, placing a sleek tablet on the table between them. His grey eyes locked onto hers, steady and unyielding. "First, allow me to apologise for the outcome of your KOSI application. Your qualifications were exemplary."

Selest stiffened. "Exemplary? Then why—"

He raised a hand, cutting her off. "Because *I* ensured you wouldn't be selected."

Her breath caught. "You . . . what?"

"My name is Dominic Veir. I am one of the directors of the Eternum Project."

Selest's eyes widened. "No way! That mission started in the year 3328 and was abandoned twenty years ago. It was condemned – the mass production of non-viable synthetic humans was deemed unethical, and the production of biological Loaders was . . . unfeasible."

"Condemned only by the religious sects that have been sprouting up lately. They're not a threat but create enough noise to muddy public opinion. Later, we wanted the world to believe the project was dead. It's a facade that protects the most important process in human history. Eternum has been rebuilt, funded to levels you can't imagine, and it's thriving."

"Nothing to do with me." Selest grinned mockingly, sliding the meatball off her fork with her teeth. "I'm a surgeon, not a bioengineer," she added with her mouth full.

Dominic matched her grin. "We know you're both and much more. We've been monitoring you for some time, Ms Dvali. Your skills and intellect are precisely what we need for a far more critical endeavour than replacing medical staff on the KOSI station."

Selest's anger flared. "You sabotaged my application and think I'll just ... join your project?"

Dominic met her indignation with calm, calculated composure. "I didn't come here expecting an easy conversation, Ms Dvali. But I assure you, my actions were necessary. Mars and KOSI would have wasted your talents. The

Eternum Project offers something greater – a chance to reshape humanity's future."

Selest leaned back, crossing her arms. "You think that's enough to convince me? I've worked hard to get here. You had no right."

"Perhaps not," Dominic said, spreading his hands slightly. "But I had the responsibility. You've chosen your career to prepare for the extraordinary, right? Eternum is extraordinary. And more."

Selest's voice turned sharp. "What exactly are you making, then? Another generation of self-aware prototypes that live a bit longer than hamsters? And why did you trick me instead of asking outright?"

"Because Eternum requires secrecy and commitment," he said. "We couldn't risk you declining out of loyalty to your KOSI dreams. Now you have no distractions."

"I have a fiancé," Selest retorted.

Dominic frowned. "You don't. Everything we know about you is thanks to our lead researcher, Aldo Wren, who failed in only one aspect of his mission. He genuinely would have married you if we'd let him."

Selest froze, unable to move, speak or swallow the food lodged painfully in her throat. She coughed violently. In one spinning movement, she pushed the chair back with a loud bang and stumbled to her feet, swaying as she tried to distance herself from the man. "Stay away from me," she rasped, her voice trembling. Through her blurred vision, she caught a glimpse of Tessa's worried face behind the counter.

Firm hands pressed her back into the chair. Too shaken to resist, she dropped her head onto her folded arms, her breath uneven, and fury boiling inside her.

The man waited silently, his expression calm and devoid of mockery. He leaned forwards slightly, his tone solemn as he resumed speaking. "Earth is dying, Ms Dvali. You know this better than most. Mars might buy us some time, but we'll eventually face extinction. Eternum isn't just about survival on another planet – it's about evolution."

"Evolution?" she echoed bitterly. "You ruined my life for the sake of . . . evolution?"

"You know, humanity has reached a breaking point. Conventional methods won't save us. Eternum is about creating a new type of Loader, human–AI hybrids – beings with resilience, intelligence and adaptability beyond our own. They'll carry the sum of our knowledge and existence, surviving where we cannot."

Selest stared at him, disbelief and unease flickering across her face. "Hybrids? Really? You're talking about playing God."

"Not playing. Making one. I'm talking about ensuring humanity's survival, even if that means creating something almost as capable," Dominic replied. "Without Homo Deus, there won't be a future to debate morality. You'd be one of the lead architects of this evolution. Your expertise in surgery, bioengineering and applied neurotechnology is exactly what I need."

Her mind spun, her anger battling with the undeniable intrigue his words evoked. "So you sent a man to break my heart and failed my application somehow to . . . trap me?"

"To protect Eternum and to free you. From mediocrity," Dominic replied without hesitation. "From spending your brilliance on half measures and baby diapers. This project will define humanity's legacy. And you, Selest Dvali, have the chance to stand at its forefront."

Selest wanted to scream, to tell him where he could shove his offer. But a small, treacherous voice in the back of her mind whispered that he wasn't wrong.

"You sabotaged my life," she said again, her voice quieter but no less firm. "You decided for me."

"I made a choice to ensure humanity gets its best minds where they're needed most," Dominic said unapologetically. "I did my job. But deep inside, I know you would have said yes anyway, so let's skip the drama. This device will activate, responding only to your biosignature. Take it, review the information and prepare yourself. We're assembling a team of visionaries, and I want you on it. And I always get what I want."

Selest stared at the tablet, its grey surface gleaming under the café lights. It was the key to a path she hadn't chosen – but one she couldn't ignore.

Dominic stood, sensing her hesitation. "Our project isn't about taking chances, Ms Dvali. It's about creating them. You have one week to get yourself ready to go. All the details are on the tablet."

With that, he turned and left, leaving her alone. Selest's fingers hovered over the tablet as her heart pounded, her thoughts tangled. Her life had been upended in a matter of hours. But one thing was certain: nothing would ever be the same again.

2: Abeni Adesina

The day of Selest's departure carried a hint of spring, or at least the idea of it – if one squinted hard enough. The winter wind, relentless in its mission, had finally calmed. Through the murky veil of clouds, thick with the detritus of the season, a glowing patch betrayed the sun's whereabouts. It was enough to risk letting her hair down and not wearing her protective cloak with its masked hood. Selest folded it carefully into her suitcase. After all, it wasn't April yet.

Her luggage was modest in size, packed

with a careful balance of sentimentality and practicality, and she also had Mr Veir's tablet, which she would return to him. The company would provide the essentials: towels, sheets, toiletries, warm clothes, sportswear, uniforms, formal and casual wear, shoes and even household utensils. What she brought was far more personal: a turquoise dress, a keepsake of the mother she'd never known. Her grandmother once told her that it was in this dress that her mother had met her father. In her dad's memory, she kept a flat piece of well-weathered slate, intricately carved with the ruins of an ancient English castle – likely Tintagel. Her other items were equally cherished: a terminal loaded with her favourite music, her university gold medal and a black pendant with Azabache amber – but that was another story. Aldo's ruby ring remained behind, deliberately left on her flat's windowsill. Everything else she truly needed, she carried in her head.

Mr Veir had been right – what she found on the tablet had astounded her. The depth of the achievements and the sheer scope of the project left her marvelling and, for the first time since she was eight, questioning her own capabilities. It was humbling, unsettling and thrilling all at once. Upon turning twenty-seven last September, Selest began considering whether it was time to start a family – a life beyond work. That thought now seemed distant, perhaps irrelevant. A future tied to a singular path was no longer an option.

First, Selest had to fly to Ulaanbaatar to find the pickup coordinates. She felt curious when she arrived at the designated departure point. This abandoned railway station hadn't seen a train in decades. The rails had long been removed, leaving the platform to crumble into moss and weeds. Selest wore a coffee-coloured travelling suit, and her small charcoal suitcase seemed a shadow of her presence.

To her surprise, she wasn't there alone.

Another young woman stood waiting, a large suitcase beside her. She looked like a photo negative version of Selest. The two were of a similar height and build, but the stranger's skin was a deep, rich brown. Her travelling outfit was beige, and her suitcase gleamed silver. Though their fashion styles were alike, Selest's hair was a cascade of dark curls, while the stranger's sleek strands fell straight and shining, almost white with a platinum shimmer. Pale-blue eyes regarded Selest with open curiosity and a friendly glint.

The stranger spoke first, her voice smooth but edged with dry humour. "Let me guess. Michael recruited you too? Setting your house and garden on fire and making it look like an accident?"

"Something like that," Selest replied, frowning. "Only his name was Dominic."

"Wow," the woman said with a grin. "Dominic Veir himself. You must be someone important. By the way, my name is Abeni Adesina. My friends call me Ab."

Selest extended a hand. "Selest Dvali."

Abeni clasped it firmly, her grin widening. "Looks like we're in this together, Selest. Let's see where they're sending us."

Selest looked closely into Abeni's blue eyes and said, "Forgive me if I seem distrustful, but this Dominic has already sent a person to spy on me once. I have very good reason to suspect you might also be an Eternum agent."

Abeni chuckled, thought for a moment and pulled up the sleeve of her jacket. "These people are certainly capable of anything to get what they want, but not so much as to risk losing it. However, even they occasionally overdo it."

Selest, an experienced medic, knew well what real first-degree burns looked like under the transparent membrane of a dressing. You couldn't fake something like that as easily as a declaration of love.

"Yesterday I had another skin graft, so there are just bandages on my leg now," Abeni said, lowering her sleeve and touching her hip.

"Sorry," said Selest, about to express her indignation, but she heard the whirr of a thermocopter approaching.

Designed and built during the Platinum Age, such low-flying or fast all-terrain vehicles could now only be afforded by military organisations, scientific foundations and very rich eccentrics. It hovered above them for a moment and then landed on one of the empty platforms.

Both women stepped into the automatically opening door and saw two empty seats in the brightly lit interior. The other six were occupied by men and women in travelling suits, their suitcases beside them and identical expressions on their faces – a mixture of excitement and bewilderment.

The vehicle hummed to life as soon as the doors sealed shut. The air inside was filtered and crisp, contrasting with the gritty outside world. Abeni leaned back, crossing her legs with an air of nonchalance, though her fingers drummed nervously on the armrest.

"So," Selest's new friend began, her voice low. "Did Dominic tell you where we're actually going? Or is he keeping you in the dark too?"

Selest shook her head, fixing her gaze on the horizon visible through the tinted windows. "He mentioned an Eternum facility. Somewhere remote. That's all I know."

Abeni smirked. "Typical. I wouldn't expect full disclosure from them – not yet, anyway. One thing is clear: we're headed somewhere no one's supposed to know exists."

One of the other passengers, a wiry man with prematurely thinning hair, turned slightly towards them. "You've met Mr Veir?" he asked. "He recruited me too. He showed up at my lab. It was a day after mystics raided the whole building, and important equipment was destroyed. He said my work was 'too valuable to be wasted.'"

Selest raised an eyebrow. "I wouldn't be surprised if this Veir arranged that raid. But what is it that you do?"

"Neural interfacing," the man replied, a note of pride creeping into his tone. "They've got big plans for me, apparently. Something about enhancing physical resilience."

Abeni laughed softly. "Sounds like they've been pulling the same strings with all of us. Burning down our plans and then appealing to our egos and dangling the *save humanity* carrot in front of our noses."

Selest couldn't help but nod in agreement, but then she stared at the man. "Excuse me, wasn't that your paper I read in *New Science* last year? You are Shademaker, right? There was a picture, but all I remember was the beard."

"Yes, ma'am, Fred Shademaker at your service," the man said, saluting in a mock-military manner. "But I got rid of the beard long ago – it made me look old."

"I'm honoured, Genatsvale!" Selest replied, turning her swivel seat 180 degrees to face him. "I loved your theories about the multi-adaptive bio-suit. The part where you discussed integrating human metabolism with a computerised garment to collaborate in harsh conditions was immensely thought-provoking."

Fred Shademaker leaned back, a pleased smile tugging at his lips. "You actually read that section?"

"Of course," Selest said, raising her eyebrows. "Efficiency under stress – whether in the organism or machine – happens to be my area of interest. Genatsvale, your theories reminded me of something I worked on during my residency, though I could never imagine applying it to wearable tech."

Fred chuckled. "Well, I'd love to hear about that sometime. It's not often I meet someone who digs past the surface. Most people want to know how flattering the suit is to wear."

The vessel gave a jolt as it passed through the wind blast, momentarily breaking their conversation. Selest steadied herself, glancing out the window at the barren landscape stretching endlessly in every direction.

"And I know you both," a woman in her sixties announced, raising her index finger. "You're Selest Dvali, born in Gudauta." The finger swung to point at Abeni. "And you – Abbie Adesina from Missouri. You were my students, two years apart. How on earth did you manage to meet?"

Abeni's laughter rang out, bright and clear like crystal. "Five minutes ago, just outside the doors of this vessel! But, Mrs Sancho? I almost didn't recognise you with your grey hair! And I'm Abeni, not Abbie!"

Selest, too, felt a flood of familiarity and a touch of nostalgia as she remembered the strict lectures of the much-aged lady. "White suits you, Professor Sancho," she said, beaming. "It makes you look even wiser."

"Two of my brightest," the old professor noted with pride to the red-headed young man beside her. "And here they are, still finding ways to surprise me."

Abeni nudged Selest with her elbow, like a schoolgirl passing a note. "Still think I'm an agent?"

"Now I'm absolutely certain of it," Selest whispered back with a sly smile.

"*Genatsvale*? What is this word?" Abeni asked, tilting her head. "I like the sound of it. Can you call me that too?"

"If you deserve as much respect as this man – sure."

Less than two minutes had passed before everyone in the vehicle was either acquainted or reacquainted. Stories flowed easily, conversations overlapping as some passengers discovered unexpected connections. Hours on the road blurred by, broken only by two brief stops in unnamed settlements – just clusters of prefab structures, where straying beyond the designated rest zones was not advised.

"And none of us knows where we're actually going at the speed of . . . what? . . . four hundred kilometres per hour?" remarked a woman named Rokhel Alonso, voicing what had lingered in everyone's mind.

"To Siberia," said a tall man named Paul Anev, breaking the brief silence. "It is over six thousand kilometres from Ulaanbaatar and will take about fifteen hours at this speed. That I know."

"I've never been to Siberia," said the youngest passenger, a quiet girl named Suli. "I heard no one really lives there any more, even with the warming."

"There aren't any proper cities – that's true," Paul replied. "But plenty of mine workers' settlements and research stations are scattered about."

"And I thought we were going to one of the ruins from the mid-Platinum Age," said Mark, a lanky young man with a prominent nose and red hair. "One of those Resorts of Hope."

"Now, Mr Gershtein, that would be fascinating," remarked Mrs Sancho, tapping his arm with her index finger – a finger that seemed to have a life of its own, constantly poking chests, pointing, threatening and finishing other people's sentences. "There were only four of those resorts. Three are in the northern hemisphere, and one is in southern Australia. I've always wanted to see one."

When everyone grew weary from the journey and drifted off to nap in their adjustable seats, Selest found herself deep in thought. It all made sense really. A resort far removed from civilisation could still have expansive underground facilities. Its equipment might be outdated, but it would have been state of the art in its time, rich with resources and infrastructure. Although Mr Veir, most likely, could afford some upgrades. There would be living quarters designed to accommodate hundreds of trainees and staff. Not many people knew the exact coordinates of such places, which were hidden even from satellite detection. And as for the religious activists? They wouldn't stand a chance of reaching it unless they came from Alaska or further east.

Selest permitted herself a faint smile of excitement and worry. Fortified by secrecy and inaccessibility, a remote location like that seemed the perfect place for whatever this mission entailed. The vehicle's hum was steady, almost hypnotic, and she wondered briefly what secrets and surprises the Platinum Age ruins might hold.

3: Ozhogino

The landscape that stretched before them was a far cry from the lush "land of lakes" it had once been. Now there was only a single, meagre lake south-east of the towering mountain, its waters dark and still, reflecting the overcast sky. The air carried a biting chill – not quite Siberian winter, but a stark reminder of Earth's dwindling resources. Snow was a rarity these days; it seemed the planet could no longer spare enough water for such extravagance.

Through the thermocopter's reinforced windows, they glimpsed scattered remnants of a forgotten age – crumbling buildings with rusted skeletons, their facades pockmarked by time and weathering. Towering radio antennae loomed over the wasteland like ancient sentinels, one still operational, its massive dish angled skyward in quiet defiance. They had passed a few wind generators at several points along their journey, and these spun wildly, their desperate energy harvesting a mere whisper of the power once needed to sustain a civilisation.

A low thrum reverberated through their bones when the thermocopter finally touched down on the sandlot. As soon as the passengers disembarked, the vehicle lifted off again, its departure stirring a brief cloud of dust before vanishing into the grey sky.

They were met by Dominic Veir, who stood at the head of a small welcoming party. Dominic, flanked by two assistants dressed in identical black utility suits, expressed measured enthusiasm. "Welcome to Ozhogino, home of Eternum," he said, his voice carrying easily over the desolate silence.

The name tugged at something deep within Selest. Not many people remember the true significance of places like this. Ages ago, these so-called Resorts of Hope had been more than relics; they had been hallowed ground, the breeding and training sites for the first wave of colonists who had set out for the distant constellation of Lyra.

Mr Veir wasted no time ushering them inside, leading them through the dilapidated building crowned by the only functioning dish. A rusted sign, half-buried in sand, flaked away as they passed – a silent relic of what once was. The lift, creaking and groaning under their weight, carried them deep underground.

As they descended, Fred Shademaker broke the heavy silence with a chuckle. "So," he said, leaning against the lift's panel, "are we excited, nervous or both?"

Selest smirked faintly, glancing back at him. "I can only speak for myself. Let's say . . . I don't need a bio-suit to keep my heart rate elevated right now."

Fred laughed, rubbing his chin where his old beard used to be. "Fair enough. Let's just hope Mr Veir didn't oversell this whole 'Eternum' business. Otherwise, we might all need those suits sooner than we think."

The next task was for all of them to rest from the long and tiring journey. Abeni had hinted, with a hopeful grin, that she and Selest could be room-mates, but the facility was vast – capable of housing hundreds – so everyone was assigned a private space. Selest found hers to be functional but comfortable, with a bed that was almost too soft after the rough journey. The room was minimalist, with smooth walls and a single artificial window displaying a backlit photographic image from centuries past – a snow-covered pine forest. As described in the instructions, the generously sized wardrobe was stocked with everything she might need, and all the clothes were perfectly her size. A small desk and an embedded screen blinked gently, awaiting her input. She dropped her suitcase by the door and collapsed onto the bed, staring at the ceiling, letting the silence settle around her. Thoughts swarmed in her head, jostling for space, forming a disorderly queue, until she shut her eyes and told them all to leave her alone for a few hours.

The following morning, they gathered in the mess hall for an incredibly superfluous breakfast with Dominic Veir. The long steel table was laden with an impressive variety of food – fresh fruit, warm pastries, eggs prepared in more ways than reasonable, and a choice of drinks ranging from freshly brewed coffee to colourful berries and herbal infusions. The spread was almost suspiciously lavish.

After spooning a generous portion of pâté d'oie onto her plate, Abeni leaned closer to Selest and murmured, "Feels a bit too good to be true, doesn't it?"

Selest nodded, stirring her coffee thoughtfully. "Either they really want us to feel at home ... or they're compensating for something."

As if sensing the undercurrent of scepticism, Dominic raised his glass of sparkling water. "To new beginnings," he said with a smile that didn't quite reach his eyes. "You deserve a bit of comfort after such a long trip."

The atmosphere remained light over steaming plates of food, but an undercurrent of anticipation lingered. Conversations went on in earnest, voices blending with the low hum of the ventilation system. Paul Anev talked at length about his research on cryogenic adaptations, while Fred Shademaker chimed in with musings on bio-engineered perspectives. Selest, ever observant, noticed Dominic watching them closely as if measuring their reactions.

After breakfast, Mr Veir led them on a tour of the working laboratories. As they walked through sterile hallways, past rooms humming with technology, it became increasingly clear that something was ... off. They saw only a handful of people – a few dozen technical staff, security personnel stationed at key points, and medical technicians attending to various tasks. Beyond them, the facility was eerily quiet.

Abeni lagged behind Selest. "I expected a buzzing hive of activity. This place could house hundreds, but where is everyone?"

Selest pursed her lips. "Maybe we're early arrivals. Or maybe . . . we're the only ones Eternum needs."

Dominic paused before a set of reinforced glass doors and gestured inside. "Welcome to your new workplace," he announced, his voice echoing in the cavernous room beyond. Inside, rows of workstations gleamed under bright artificial light and complex machinery, blinking with status indicators, lined the walls.

"You'll find everything you need here, including the project objectives," Dominic continued smoothly. "Cutting-edge tools, unrestricted research access, and, of course, complete discretion."

"Discretion?" Fred raised an eyebrow. "Mustn't we sign something?"

Dominic smiled thinly. "You'll understand soon enough. For now, take your time exploring. Settle in. Work begins tomorrow." With that, he turned on his heel and strode off, leaving them to take in the eerie emptiness of their new surroundings.

Abeni crossed her arms, watching him go. "I don't like this," she muttered.

Selest exhaled slowly. "Neither do I. He's not telling us something. Let's take a look at those objectives—"

The worried voice of Professor Mel Sancho interrupted her. "Where is that young girl? Suli . . . I saw her coming for breakfast but not after."

"And the red-headed Israeli is also gone," added Fred Shademaker. "What's his name? Mark?"

It was true. As soon as Dominic and his assistant left, they discovered there were only six of them now.

"I'm sure there's nothing to worry about," Paul Anev said. "Didn't you see that they flirted with each other all the way here? I don't know where they are now, but I can easily imagine what they're doing."

"Didn't our young talent want to know where we all will work?" Selest mused.

The skinny woman, Rokhel, shrugged. "The girl told me she's not a scientist. She's an orphan from Oslo's sports college. She had no idea why she was chosen to work here."

"And the boy is from the military academy. I guess he's here to work as a guard. Maybe he'll guard *us* so *we* don't escape." Abeni's joke fell flat. No one even smiled.

"I can't take this disappearance lightly," Professor Sancho muttered, crossing her arms tightly. "Even if it's just young love blooming."

Selest glanced at Abeni, who had the same wary expression. "We don't really know or understand this place yet. Surely, they wouldn't bring those two here to be harmed. Let's wait and start learning what we're here for. So far, everything I've seen on Dominic's tablet was very promising."

Fred rubbed his chin and walked over to his workstation. "I agree. I don't like unknown variables in places like this, but we have a job to do."

The others followed his lead, and soon everyone was absorbed in the initial research plans, adapting their roles to the available resources and proposed implementation strategies.

Selest was the first to break the silence, her voice sharp with indignation. "What? All subjects must be cloned here? I thought we would work with adult volunteers!"

To her surprise, no one reacted with the same shock. Instead, her colleagues remained silent, their heads bowed as if they had already reached the same grim conclusion.

Finally, Abeni spoke, her voice barely above a whisper. "It's worse than I thought. I'll have to grow cloned embryos in artificial wombs. They've got an entire gallery of the latest models here." She paused, her expression darkening. "Guess whose biomaterial they want me to use."

Selest's palms grew clammy with the terrible realisation.

The tension in the data room was suffocating. Eyes flickered over screens, and glances were exchanged, but no one dared speak first. The weight of what they had just learned hung heavy in the air. Selest's face was pale, her jaw clenched so tightly it hurt. Abeni sat frozen, staring at the blinking text on her screen, while Fred and Rokhel exchanged uneasy sighs.

Selest pushed her seat back violently, the screech echoing through the room. Without a word, she stormed out. The heavy doors slid open, then shut quickly. No staff tried to stop her. The sterile corridors of the facility blurred as she strode through them, her heart pounding with anger and disbelief. She needed to find Dominic Veir. Now. Her new colleagues just managed to keep up.

She found him in the expansive lobby of the medical wing, standing still with an air of infuriating calm as though he had expected her all along. The high ceilings and stark white walls did little to muffle her voice as she shouted, her rage finally unleashed.

"Hey, Veir! You left out some quite crucial details! Didn't you?" she spat. "You conveniently omitted the fact that two of our so-called colleagues are nothing more than gamete donors! Carefully selected for their genetic material, as if they're livestock!"

Dominic's expression remained calm, his hands folded neatly behind his back.

"Ms Dvali," he said in that maddeningly composed voice of his, "I assure you, they were under no pressure to come here. They agreed to take an offer. Their choices led them to sign the consent form willingly."

Selest's eyes blazed. "Choices? You call this a choice? Being cornered into selling their bodies for your damned project? And Suli – she's a child, Dominic!"

"She's eighteen," he corrected. "And she will be well compensated. Her future is secured, and she will even retain one of her ovaries. We're not monsters, Selest."

"Oh, well, thank heavens for your generosity!" she snapped, sarcasm dripping from every word. "And what about the babies, Dominic? The dozens of babies you expect us to grow? That hasn't been done since the Platinum Age's demographic boost, and even then, parents had control; they had a say and brought them up. But now? Now you expect us to create human life just to experiment on it?" She took a step closer, eyes locked onto his. "Cyborg babies, Dominic? Is that the plan?"

Dominic's expression finally hardened, his patience wearing thin. "Not cyborgs, Selest. Loaders! They will be enhanced, not experimented on. And we're ensuring the survival of humanity. This is bigger than your moral dilemmas. We called out for young descendants of those few unique participants in Kepler's Object of Special Interest who chose to stay on Earth instead of travelling to Lyra. Only five responded, and only these two qualified. They all have the necessary and rare traits no one else in the world has."

"Unacceptable!" Selest hissed. "I won't be a part of this. I'm leaving."

Behind her, Abeni spoke up, her voice steady but filled with resolve. "I'm with her. I didn't sign up for this, Mr Veir. I want out."

Mr Veir said nothing to that. The others – Fred, Rokhel, Paul and even Professor Sancho – remained silent, their expressions inscrutable. Some avoided eye contact entirely.

Dominic Veir exhaled slowly, as if preparing for this reaction. He stepped to the side and activated the large wall screen with a device on his wrist. It displayed a news bulletin, stark headlines scrolling across the bottom.

Tragic Accident at the Commercial Concilium Claims Lives of Researchers and Personnel –

No Survivors.

Selest's breath caught in her throat. The screen showed their faces; all six were listed among the deceased. Her hands trembled slightly as she scanned the report: every name there, every detail meticulously fabricated.

"You see, Ms Dvali," Dominic said softly. "There is no going back. As far as the world is concerned, you are all dead. There is nothing left for you out there."

Selest felt her knees weaken, but she refused to show it. "You think this will keep us here? You think this is enough?"

"Selest, each of you has a role, and I have

one too. And, like it or not, we have a plan in place. I am willing to take responsibility for my methods of making sure you do your part. This . . . is mine."

He turned to the group, his voice taking on an authoritative edge. "Professor Sancho and Miss Adesina, you will oversee the growth and delivery of our subjects. Professor Shademaker and Miss Alonso, your focus will remain on the technology. Dr Dvali and Dr Anev – you will be responsible for putting the first and second together and ensuring a successful outcome. I have dozens of well-trained, experienced nurses and technicians to assist you when needed." He paused, letting the weight of his words sink in. "Is it all clear?"

Selest stared at him, disgust and anger twisting inside her. "You are a madman!"

"Maybe," Dominic replied seriously. "But you're visionaries. And visionaries know when they're out of options and must do what is right for all."

Selest's fists clenched at her sides, but she refused to let him see how much his words affected her. She turned on her heel and stormed out, her boots echoing down the corridor.

Behind her, Abeni followed without a word.

4: Protestants

A month had now passed since Selest and Abeni made their silent protest. They expected consequences, some form of punishment – a reduction in food, restrictions on their movements or even isolation. But none came, although they could not leave. Instead, their lives remained as on the day of their arrival. They could wander the expansive tunnels and halls of these mostly underground facilities, learn more about the project, partake in meals and entertainment, and even maintain their fitness in the gym and swimming pool. Only the elevator remained powered down, unused, sealed behind heavy security gates.

When Selest suggested during dinner that they should refuse to indulge in the luxuries provided by Eternum, Abeni shrugged and scooped another generous portion of delicacies onto her plate.

"Why?" Abeni said, chewing defiantly. "We are prisoners of a rich man who took everything from us. I will stuff myself with this caviar at his expense now."

Selest shook her head, taking a bite of her modest egg sandwich. "Ab, you're doing exactly what he wants you to do."

"He wants me to work, but I won't. It's Sancho who's pumping poor Suli with you-know-what hormones. Not me! When the girl starts hyper-ovulating, Sancho will do the egg extraction alone. Without me! Remember, Selest, we don't owe him anything. He owes us."

Selest frowned, staring at the extravagant spread of food before them. "Eat enough of this caviar, and you'll definitely owe him."

Abeni chuckled drily. "It depends on how many kilograms of rare food I value my destroyed property, my freedom and plans for the future. Sel, I wanted to travel around the world while it still exists, have a kid and grow new species of limes and other fruits for space stations."

Selest fell silent, contemplating Abeni's words. Finally, she said, "Have a child? Oh, trust me, I get that. We need to get away from here."

"I'd love that, but where to?" Abeni asked, pushing her plate aside. "Didn't you check the MESH maps? We're surrounded by hundreds of kilometres of empty tundra, where the temperature won't rise above zero until

June. Even if we're lucky with the weather and walk straight south, reaching the Bela-Gora mines or other inhabited areas will take weeks, not days. We'll freeze and starve before we make it. If you steal one of their vehicles . . . maybe then."

But Selest wasn't deterred. Over the following days, she persuaded Abeni to at least prepare for the possibility. They started small, taking long-storage snacks from the communal dining area back to their rooms: a few crackers here, a handful of nuts there. Pieces of smoked meats were wrapped in a serviette, then tucked discreetly into their pockets. Fruits were carefully dried using the automatic hairdryers in their personal bathrooms. Bit by bit, they built a stockpile, hoping it would be enough to sustain them, should they attempt an escape.

Their efforts to rally others, however, were met with disappointment. Their fellow captives had already accepted their fates.

Professor Sancho dismissed them with a weary sigh. "I'm too old to fight this, girls. What would I do out there? Die on the road? No, I'll stay."

Rokhel Alonso, a pragmatic scientist and an engineer, shrugged. "In a few years, my work here will be done. I'll leave with a hefty balance in my bank account and start over at fifty."

Paul Anev seemed almost content with their imprisonment. "I like it here," he admitted. "I don't have to worry about anything but my work. My clothes are washed, the food is cooked for me . . . And no nagging wife or mother to drill my ears! It's comfortable like nowhere else I've lived."

The inventor Fred Shademaker, however, struck a different chord. His eyes lit up when Selest challenged his complacency. "You don't understand," he told her during one of the meals. "Before this, I lacked the materials and resources to demonstrate my bio-suit to my peers. But here" – he leaned forwards, excitement lacing his voice – "here, I've started four new and very promising prototypes. The possibilities are endless."

Selest thought a moment. *And here, you have no peers to demonstrate your work to,* she almost said, but her scepticism wavered as a very special interest took hold.

"Prototypes?" she asked aloud. "What kind? Genatsvale, what progress have you made?"

Fred's chest puffed up with pride. "I've refined the metabolic integration system, enhanced adaptability to extreme environments, and improved the interface to near-instantaneous response time. It's revolutionary work, Doctor. Something I could never have achieved outside this place."

As he spoke, Selest's mind raced. Fred's work could be the key to their escape. If his bio-suits could withstand extreme conditions, they could survive the frozen wasteland outside this golden cage.

"Genatsvale, have you tested any of them for prolonged exposure to sub-zero temperatures?" she asked, trying to keep her tone casual.

Fred stroked his chin thoughtfully. "Not extensively, but theoretically they should provide sufficient insulation and metabolic support. Why?"

Abeni, catching on, nudged Selest under the table. "We're just curious," she interjected, "and humbled by your achievements."

Fred grinned, oblivious to their underlying intentions. "If you're interested, I can show you my work in progress. It's stored in the lab. You'll be impressed, I'm sure."

Over the next few days, Selest and Abeni found themselves drawn deeper into Fred's work. They observed his designs, asked questions and even assisted with tests under the guise of professional interest. In reality, they learned the suit's capabilities, searching for flaws or limitations that could impact an escape attempt.

Meanwhile, they continued stockpiling food and supplies while maintaining an air of indifference to avoid suspicion. If they could be called that, the guards, looking all the same in those uniforms and screened helmets, paid little attention to their activities, probably trusting in the facility's isolation to deter escape attempts. It was also important for Abeni's burns to heal completely so that she was well enough to travel.

Late one evening, Selest came to change her dressings, and in the privacy of her quarters, Abeni whispered, "So, what do you think? Could those bio-suits get us through the tundra?"

Selest hesitated. "Maybe. But we'd need

to take two without being noticed – and we've no idea how long the power supply would hold in real conditions. Out there, the ZPE veins in the fabric won't have much to draw from beyond kinetic energy. If we stop walking for too long . . . we might freeze."

Abeni sighed. "I see your point. The dynamo charges should give us just enough – if we keep moving. I'm worried about stopping to rest too. It's a risk, but it's better than wasting away here."

Selest nodded. "We'll keep gathering supplies. And in the meantime, we'll learn everything we can about this place. If there's even the slightest chance – we'll take it."

Their quiet rebellion continued, unnoticed by others. Each day, they edged closer to their goal, their determination growing stronger with each passing moment. The tundra above the facility's walls remained a formidable challenge.

In the meantime, they were on strike and had to find something else to do to combat their boredom.

The old library was tucked away in the farthest wing of the facility, hidden behind thick frosted glass doors that whispered open as Selest and Abeni approached. Rows of shelves stretched towards the ceiling, packed tightly with books made from synthetic polymer and even a few genuine paper volumes – relics from a time before digitisation had swallowed most written records. Abeni glanced around, her fingers skimming the spines.

"Rokhel wasn't lying," Selest murmured, trailing beside her. "This place is incredible. I remember the initial info on Dominic's Eternum tablet said that we would gain access to one of the most complete libraries outside the MESH, but I didn't believe it."

Abeni didn't respond. She'd frozen mid-step, her eyes fixed on a figure in the far corner of the room. A tall, broad-shouldered guard stood by one of the shelves, flipping through an old manual. He'd removed his helmet to read, revealing a bald head and neatly trimmed beard. Selest sensed the mood change immediately.

"Ab? What is it?"

But Abeni took a slow, deliberate step forwards, then another and then sprinted.

"Michael! Son of a—" Abeni's voice cracked like a whip across the quiet library, and the bald man's head jerked up in surprise. Before he could react, she was nearly upon him, fury blazing in her eyes.

Two staff members happened to be nearby and lunged at Abeni just in time, grabbing her by the waist and arms and holding her back as she thrashed and struggled against their grip.

"Do you know how long it took my family to grow those trees?" she shouted, her voice raw with rage. "That greenhouse – I built it with my own hands, you bastard!"

Michael stood frozen, his mouth opening and closing, his eyes wide with something that might have been regret. He took a cautious step back, his hands raised in surrender.

"I . . . I didn't have a choice, Abeni—"

"Liar!" she spat, still straining against her captors. "I know you did it! It was you! You burned my grandfather's cottage to the ground! My garden! My home! Everything!"

"Please, listen—" Michael's face was pale. "It wasn't by my will, I swear!"

Selest stepped forwards, touched Abeni's shoulder and spoke softly. "Don't, Ab. You're not completely healed yet. Let's go."

Breathing heavily, Abeni finally stopped struggling, but her glare could have burned holes through steel. The staff released their grip cautiously, standing by in case she lunged again. With one final glare at Michael, Abeni turned and stormed out of the library, Selest following close behind.

Abeni's voice came low and tight as they marched through the dim corridor.

"You have such nice little things from your past life on your shelf," she said without turning around – not out of bitterness, just quiet resignation. "It may not be much, but it's something. A connection. Me? Aside from my modest account, I lost everything that day."

She stopped so abruptly that Selest nearly collided with her. Abeni turned, eyes shining with something brittle and dangerous.

"Do you know what else I have left?" she asked. "Here. Look."

She reached beneath her collar and pulled out a small pendant on a thin chain. It was plain and cheap but heavy in her hand. With a click, she opened it.

Selest expected a photo. A lock of hair. Something nostalgic. But inside, nestled like a secret, was a translucent greenish capsule. Not medicine.

Adieu. An euthanasia pill.

Selest recognised it instantly. It was a controlled compound prescribed only to centenarians tired of living or patients whose brain function had irreversibly shut down.

It was death in its most merciful form – legally sanctioned during the Platinum Age, irreversibly final.

"Where did you get this?" Selest asked quietly.

"Stole it," Abeni said, as if recounting someone else's crime. "Back when I was in the hospital. I thought I couldn't stop the pain. All of it. It's one thing to treat burns. Another thing to survive them. Painkillers didn't help. Not even the military-grade ones. But it was *my* hospital. I did my internship there. I knew where they kept everything." She stared at the capsule, then clicked the pendant shut. "And then Veir's invitation came, and I changed my mind." She slipped the chain back under her collar. "Now I keep it to remind myself: if it ever gets bad again, *really* bad – the last choice will be mine. And mine alone." She glanced at Selest. "You won't tell anyone, will you?"

Before Selest could answer, Abeni turned and walked on, her steps calm and composed this time.

But Selest couldn't move. Not for a long minute.

Three days passed, and the ugly incident still hung over them like a storm cloud. Abeni was unusually quiet. Selest knew better than to press her.

Then, one afternoon, Michael approached them while they sat in the glass-walled room with a Japanese sand garden. He held a small potted plant awkwardly, shifting his weight from foot to foot. Abeni tensed at the sight of him.

"What do you want?" she asked flatly, her eyes narrowing.

Michael cleared his throat and extended the plant towards her. "A peace offering," he said. "I know ... I know I can't undo what happened, but I swear I – I was following orders."

Abeni didn't take the plant pot. "Orders. Of course. That makes it fine, doesn't it? Get lost."

Michael exhaled, looking genuinely hurt, but set the plant on the bench beside her. "At least keep this. It's, uh ... something to grow. Something new."

Selest leaned forwards, inspecting the green leaves. "What is it? It looks like a citrus. Maybe lime."

Abeni's brow furrowed. "Hang on ... How did he know I wanted to grow limes?"

Michael's expression faltered. "I ... I might have overheard."

Abeni crossed her arms. "Overheard who? Me? Selest?"

Selest's gaze shifted between them. "You did mention it at lunch, Ab," she said carefully. "Remember? You only recognised this man in the library because he didn't have his hat on."

Abeni's expression softened momentarily, but doubt still lingered in her eyes. "Yeah. I didn't see him there. Perhaps. Or maybe someone's been listening a little too closely. What else did you . . . overhear?"

Michael raised his hands in defence. "I swear I was just passing by. Yesterday we drove to the trading post for supplies, and I saw this plant in one of the mobile stores. That's all. Look . . . I'll leave you alone. Just . . . think about what I said."

He turned and walked away, leaving Abeni staring at the small pot. She didn't touch it for a long moment, then finally reached out, running her fingers over the smooth, waxy leaves.

"What do you think, Sel?" she asked quietly. "Michael responded to the ad that spring, and I hired him as a gardener to help me out. It's possible I told him about limes then. He was good. He acted as if he loved plants and . . . oh, shit! It was all fake! Fake like those windows in our rooms." And she sighed heavily.

Selest shrugged. "Yes, it was. But I think it's a beautiful and innocent living thing. And I think you should keep it."

Abeni sighed again, her lips curling into a reluctant smile. "Maybe. I will call it . . . Lia. But if I find out he was eavesdropping on us, he's getting this plant back. With the pot. Thrown at his head."

"Fair enough." Selest chuckled, turned serious, and added, "So, they go out for supplies. Driving what? I wonder what other transport they have here apart from thermocopters?"

Soon Lia, the real plant, sat on Abeni's fake windowsill, a small reminder of her past amid the sterile environment of her present. The young woman tended to it with quiet devotion, watering it and carefully choosing its position to catch the most of the artificial light. And yet Selest knew they could not take it with them when they left.

The incident in the library stirred something inside Selest. She sensed stronger than ever why they needed to escape. Every interaction, favour, apology and carefully chosen word from their captors only reinforced the truth: no matter how luxurious their prison, it was still a prison, and escape was the only option.

5: An Attempt

Selest examined Abeni carefully, her fingers gently tracing the vast scars on Abeni's arms and legs. Apart from the redness of the new skin, her friend was well enough, strong enough. They were ready.

For weeks, both women had thrown themselves into relentless preparation, seizing every moment to study their surroundings and gather supplies. By making an unexpected ally in Michael, Abeni had learned the hidden routes to the surface and secured access to the garage. Now, with a triumphant smirk, she held a small black cylinder up in front of Selest's nose.

"He tricked me, and now I have no problem doing the same to him," she said, dangling the stolen tag before Selest's eyes.

Selest frowned, inspecting the tiny device. "This is risky, Ab. If he realises —"

"He won't. Trust me, he's too busy trying to redeem himself." Abeni stuffed the tag into her pocket. "Let's not waste any more time."

The day of their escape finally arrived. Rokhel had a hangover – courtesy of Selest's little drinking challenge the night before – so Fred inevitably asked them both to help in the lab, running liquid fabric tests and analysing the efficiency of the sweat recycling mechanisms.

Fred, bless him, was a proper scientific genius – brilliant but hopelessly single-minded. Once immersed in his calculations, the entire world could crumble around him, and he'd still be oblivious. As expected, he barely noticed when both women left the lab. They were wearing bio-suits concealed beneath their tracksuits, the electronically enhanced fabric pressing snugly against their skin.

They went to their rooms, waited for nightfall and then regrouped by the lift shaft. Both had rolled-up blankets and suitcases full of food, medical supplies and other things they did not want to leave behind. Both wore their fur parkas and boots, meant for the rare but precious walks outside their prison, permitted twice a month. The facility's lights were already dimmed for the evening, shadows stretching long across the cold polymer floors. They slipped through the empty hallways unnoticed, their steps silent. They reached the lift without incident, pausing before the unguarded sealed door. The security tag worked, and the iron net shifted aside.

"All set?" Selest whispered.

Abeni nodded. "Let's do this."

Selest hesitated, her pulse hammering in her ears. "This feels . . . too easy."

Abeni forced a grin. "Let's not question our luck."

The lift ascended with a soft hum, and they soon found themselves inside the bleak concrete shell of the surface outpost. A wave of biting cold wrapped around them the moment they stepped outside. The suits responded almost instantly, the internal heating systems kicking in. The icy wind, however, still gnawed at their exposed faces.

"Look!" Abeni pointed excitedly to the row of vehicles in the garage. "We have options."

Selest scanned the choices – transport rovers and sleek quad bikes with helmets on their seats. "I don't know how to drive these."

Abeni smirked. "Lucky for you, I do. I am a country girl. Just put your 'bonnet' on, my lady, and hold tight. These things are very fast."

She bypassed the ignition with deft fingers, and the quad bike roared to life beneath them. They sped off across the frozen wasteland, the wind whipping against their visors. Hope surged in Selest's chest, but it was short-lived.

Barely a couple of hours into their escape, the low hum of a thermocopter cut through the roar of their engine. Selest's heart sank the instant before a sniper's shot silently sliced through the bike's tyres with a power ray. The vehicle skidded out of control, hurling them into deep, frozen ash left behind by the long-burned taiga. The ash received them with a loud crunch, softening their fall. If not for the layers of clothing wrapped around them, they wouldn't have survived the impact.

"Damn it!" Abeni cursed, struggling to her feet once they stopped rolling. "Are you all right?"

Selest clutched her arm, her mind racing.

"I think so. Dominic . . . he knew. He was toying with us! Now he thinks we will turn back!"

Abeni set her jaw, watching the disappearing thermocopter's light in the distance, an orange star against the dark sky. "We're not giving up. We walk. We probably gained hundreds of kilometres anyway on that thing."

They took what they could from the crashed bike and fashioned a makeshift cart. Harnessing themselves to it, they pressed on. It was better than carrying their luggage. The landscape was hostile yet reasonably level, littered with the skeletal remains of low-growing trees, dried by the wind and frost to ringing, bone-like whiteness. From time to time, Selest gathered branches for campfires, storing them in the cart alongside chunks of ice chipped from the dents in the frozen ground.

They trudged forwards, the tundra stretching endlessly in all directions. Now and then, they stopped to rest, huddling for warmth, sharing carefully rationed food. The mugs they'd stolen from the resort, used in the workplace to reheat cold tea and coffee, now served to melt ice for drinking.

But after some time, Selest noticed a change in her friend.

"Ab, you're slowing down. What's wrong?"

Abeni hesitated, then sighed. "I think the fall damaged my suit. It's not regulating heat properly."

"Why didn't you tell me sooner? We need to swap and —"

"No," Abeni interrupted firmly. "You need your suit. If we try to share, we'll both freeze. Let's just keep moving. It's not too bad when we do."

Hours passed, and Abeni's strength waned with every step. Her breath came in ragged gasps, her movements sluggish. Selest decided it was time to stop when she spotted a large crack in the earth – wide enough to shelter them from the wind and build a fire at its base. But the flames were pitiful against the relentless cold. She burned every branch she gathered, even sacrificing parts of her luggage for warmth, including books and her mother's dress. Abeni, wrapped in all the blankets they had, murmured that she could no longer feel her toes.

Selest huddled close to her, voice trembling. "We should turn back. Try to—"

"No!" Abeni insisted, eyes wild with determination. "Sel . . . I can't go back. I won't."

"Ab, what is it you are not telling me?"

Abeni's mouth curled into a faint smile, her eyelids lowering. "Selest . . . you have to go on without me. You still have a chance. I'll only slow you down."

"No," Selest snapped. "We should go back. We'll take turns in the suit if we must –

sleep in shifts, rely on fire, stretch the rations, melt ice for water. Even if it takes a week, we'll make it. Don't start that leave-me-behind talk."

"Back? For my sake? No." Abeni's voice was soft. "Go forwards, Sel. Your plan might still work – but not for me. It's too late."

"What are you saying? You have to survive. We'll try again – escape Eternum, find a quiet place, grow things, rebuild . . . fall in love again—"

"I already have," Abeni said. Her voice was thin but steady. "I've been in love with you, Selest. All this time."

Selest froze. "What?"

"It doesn't matter now. I'm not dying from the cold. It's internal bleeding – I can feel it. I'm a doctor too, remember?" Her voice dropped to a hush. "Just . . . give me a kiss, will you? This is goodbye."

Selest couldn't speak. The tears on her cheeks froze in place.

"Stay with me, Ab," she whispered at last, "Genatsvale."

She cupped Abeni's face with a trembling hand and leaned in. Her full lips felt soft, cold and final.

Moments later, Abeni's body went limp, and Selest let out a strangled sob as she rocked her gently. The loneliness was suffocating. She had never felt so helpless in her life.

In her grief, she was ready to surrender, to let the cold take her too, but the relentless drone of the thermocopter returned.

Selest did not remember what happened next. She was dragged back into its metallic grasp, screaming and struggling against the men in darkened polymer visors. One tried to offer her a flask of something hot, but she shoved him away and struck his faceless mask with all her might. Then she begged them not to leave Abeni behind, but exhaustion consumed her. At some point, she fainted, lost in unbearable fatigue and grief.

Selest woke to the facility's sterile light and Professor Mel Sancho's stony face. The old woman's hands were clasped tightly behind her back. She was clearly not as friendly as before, and when Selest tried to ask questions, she simply turned away, leaving her in silence.

Selest recovered quickly, or at least her tired and bruised body did. The moment she was well enough, she went straight to Abeni's room, half expecting – half hoping – to find her there. But the room was empty, stripped of all traces of Abeni's existence. The bed was neatly made, the shelves bare. Only the little plant remained, its leaves drooping slightly in the dim artificial light.

Selest touched the edge of the pot, swallowing the ache in her throat.

The next day, Dominic came. He stood in Selest's doorway, arms folded, his eyes cold and unyielding. "Abeni is gone," he said without preamble, his voice sharp and final. "And you have no one to blame but yourself."

He let the words settle between them like ballast, then added, "You'd do well to stop sacrificing people's lives for your personal standards and start making yourself useful for humanity's future."

Selest said nothing. She didn't see him, didn't flinch. Her stare felt hollow, fixed somewhere beyond him, beyond the walls, beyond everything.

Later that day, she saw Fred in the dining hall, his kind face offering a brief flicker of something like normality. He was the only one who still spoke to her without judgement. His eyes lit up with something close to excitement as he spotted her. "You actually took the suits out there?" he asked, leaning in eagerly. "Yours was still working when they brought it back to me. Fascinating! The data we've collected – it's invaluable."

He patted her shoulder absent-mindedly, oblivious to the state of her, to the grief clawing at her insides. She stared at him for a long moment, feeling neither anger nor comfort. She knew now – Fred's mind worked differently, untouched by human loss. Without a word, she left him and returned to her quarters. The little potted plant sat on her bedside table now. She cradled it gently in her hands, tracing the delicate veins of its leaves with a trembling finger.

"I'll take care of Lia, Ab," she whispered. "I promise."

6: Redemption

At first, everyone was cold towards Selest. Perhaps they had been told the story of the escape procession, a version in which she had not come across as very appealing. She still refused to work, but now she spent most of her time in her room or the library. It was there, about a week after her return, that Paul Anev approached and sat down beside her.

"Selest," he began after a long silence, "I've been trying to cope with our task alone. I thought I could achieve the aimed-for results without you, but our subjects grow quickly, and I am afraid—"

"You needn't continue." She interrupted him, her tone cool. "If Dominic thinks I feel guilty enough to be spurred into work to restore your goodwill towards me, he is mistaken. I am a hermit by nature; I don't need friends. And I feel no guilt."

Paul shook his head earnestly. "Our goodwill towards you? Selest, one of the guards told us that it was Mr Veir who ordered them to shoot the bike and abandon Abeni in the tundra. You're not to blame for her death. It was him and his ways of leading Eternum. And we were told to stay away from you so you wouldn't bring trouble upon us too. But we're not children. We understand everything. And I really need your help."

"With what?"

"Installing platinum contacts to connect the central nervous system with the implant for an additional database in an organism that is still growing. The wires don't stretch as a tissue grows – you know that."

"There's no way," Selest replied flatly. "You can place the implant in the organism, not the wired contact system. That is only possible once the subject is fully grown."

"But we want the brain to develop with the prefix already installed."

"Then let it remain external for the necessary period, until we find out how to do it wirelessly."

Anev's face lit up. "Brilliant."

Selest nodded. "And which guard told you about Abeni? Michael?"

"No. He is not around any more. I think he left . . . or was kicked out."

She narrowed her eyes, intrigued. "Then who?"

Paul hesitated. "It doesn't matter now. What matters is that we need to move forwards, and I can't do it without you."

Selest studied him, weighing his sincerity. Eventually, she sighed. "I'll think about it."

Later, she walked through the quiet corridors of the facility, the sterile scent of filters making the air almost natural. She made her way to the gallery of artificial wombs, where the soft hum of machinery accompanied the rhythmic pulsing of nutrient fluids circulating through the chambers. The sight was fascinating and unsettling – row upon row of developing foetuses, each suspended in its self-contained world, tiny bodies forming behind the small observation windows.

She barely took it all in when she noticed a familiar figure nearby. Young Suli stood, gazing at one of the pods, her dark eyes filled with something that resembled both awe and trepidation. Selest hesitated, unsure whether to interrupt, but Suli seemed lost in thought, unaware of her presence.

"You're not supposed to be here," Selest finally said, her voice quiet but firm.

Suli startled, turning sharply before letting out a nervous laugh. "I know. I just . . . I wanted to see them. I thought . . . I should, before I leave."

"You're leaving?"

Suli nodded, her eyes following the rows of the artificial wombs. "Yes. Tonight. I am not needed here any more. New name, new life, lots of money." A wry smile played on her lips. "Seems like a fair trade for my dodgy past, don't you think? I was absconding. Mr Veir and this place offered me a way out. A blessing really."

Selest studied the young woman closely. There was a resolute tone in her voice, but beneath it lurked a bitterness that couldn't be ignored. She realised she didn't want to ask Suli what she had done or what she was running from. Instead, she asked, "And you're content with your role here?"

Suli's smile faded. "Content? Maybe not. But this is my chance to start again." Her eyes flickered to the pods. "How is it that all these babies are mine? I was told only one hundred and four eggs matured."

Selest stepped closer, frowning as she scanned the rows of foetuses. "Babies? You mean subjects. When your eggs were fertilised with gametes from that red-headed boy who they sent back to his academy, the resulting zygotes were treated using Professor Sancho's method." She paused. "The process forces the embryos, at their cleavage stage, to divide three or even five times before being developed into individual organisms."

Suli's expression darkened. "So there are many twins here," she said hollowly.

"Yes. Many . . . clones."

A heavy silence settled between them, broken only by the hum of the machines. Suli sighed and stepped back. "I feel like a hive queen. But it doesn't matter any more. I'll be gone soon; none of this will be my concern."

"And if it was?" Selest asked quietly.

Suli hesitated at the door, then shook her head. "It's not. Goodbye, Doctor. I am sure you will take good care of them."

She left, and Selest remained, surrounded by the silent, growing lives behind the glass. The burden of responsibility pressed on her. She had refused to work, believing her defiance to be the only resistance left. But standing here, witnessing the reality of their experiments, she began to question it all.

Hours later, when she found Paul Anev in the laboratory, she surprised even herself with her words.

"Paul, let's get to work."

From that moment, something changed. The Eternum staff became more cheerful; Selest noticed people smiling and speaking loudly in her presence again. Her days were filled with routine, meaning and achievements. She woke in the morning knowing what lay ahead and what problems she would solve.

She never knew if it was Dominic's way of rewarding her, as she had not seen him in days. But one evening, as she approached her quarters, a figure was waiting at her door. As she drew closer, he removed his visor. Recognition hit her like a blow to the chest.

His black hair was now cropped short, and his skin held that warm olive tone, like old bronze, familiar and unmistakable. It was him.

Selest felt her heart lurch, an old wound torn open by the mere sight of him.

"Selest," he said softly, his voice laden with the shadow of all that had passed.

She swallowed hard, then spoke, keeping her voice steady. "Aldo, I thought you were out in the world, recruiting more women for Eternum."

He offered a half smile, tinged with regret. "No, you were my only target."

Silence stretched between them, thick with unspoken words.

Selest crossed her arms. "What are you doing here?"

Aldo sighed, rubbing the back of his neck. "I'm working for Eternum. I'm a trading agent, and I guard transportations. I was specially assigned to get you because the AI calculated you were more likely to fall for me than any other agent. What it didn't tell me, was that it works both ways . . . I tried to keep my distance here and forget everything. Until you almost smashed my face in that thermocopter. Then I remembered how much I love you . . ."

Selest let out a bitter laugh. "Love? I was practically kidnapped, Aldo. My life was taken from me. Everything I worked for . . . destroyed."

Aldo's expression darkened. "I'm sorry,

Selest. If I had known everything—"

"Would you refuse to follow orders?" she snapped, her voice sharper than she intended.

He hesitated. "I thought you'd be safe here. You don't know what's happening in the world, Selest. There are mystics – religious sects killing scientists and burning books. That accident where you were supposed to die really did happen. We only managed to save those who went to KOSI."

Selest studied him, searching for deception but finding only honesty in his tired eyes. She sighed and leaned against the wall. "Well, I'm here now. What do you want, Aldo?"

He looked at her earnestly. "To help you. To make things ... better. Can I show you something?"

Selest shook her head. "Not now."

He took a step closer. "Please. I've been working on something for weeks. You have to see it."

Selest looked away, her mind racing. "Abeni is gone. You . . . you didn't take her that day. You left her to die."

Aldo's face fell, and he whispered, "I'm sorry. I was told she was dead already."

She shrugged, the pain still too fresh to acknowledge fully. "I don't know if I can trust you, Aldo. You tricked me once."

"And I regret it every day," he admitted. "Please, let me make up for at least one thing. Please, come."

Selest exhaled slowly, considering. "Will you leave me alone after?"

He nodded. "If you still want me to."

Selest hesitated, then spoke up. "Fine. Show me, Aldo. But don't think for a second this changes anything."

Aldo's face softened with a mix of relief and gratitude. "I wouldn't dream of it," he said, stepping aside to let her pass.

She followed him through the dimly lit corridors, past the familiar sterile halls she had grown accustomed to. As they walked in silence, Selest stole glances at him. He looked different, but there was still that unmistakable fire in his eyes, the same one that had drawn her to him a few years ago.

They reached a section of the facility she had never explored before. Aldo led her to a narrow door and pressed his palm against a biometric scanner. The door slid open with a faint hiss, revealing a small but comfortable living space inside.

Selest stepped in cautiously, her breath catching in her throat. It was her old apartment – down to the smallest detail. The adjustable walls precisely duplicated the original layout. Her furniture was in the right places, the bookshelves stacked with the titles she'd left behind – even the orange cat soft toy sat on the bedside table. The so-called window displayed a photograph of the view – so painfully familiar it made her chest tighten. Her gaze dropped to the fake windowsill, and there it was: Aldo's ring, resting exactly where she'd left it on the day she walked away.

"Aldo," she whispered, touching her favourite hairbrush, "How did you—"

"I've been working on this since you arrived," he admitted quietly. "I smuggled everything in, item by item, even your old socks and slippers. I wanted you to have something familiar that felt like home."

Selest turned to him, her expression unreadable. "Why? What's the point? It doesn't erase what happened."

"No, it doesn't," Aldo agreed. "But I thought . . . if I could give you some sense of normality, even just a little, it might help."

She sighed heavily, emotions threatening to overwhelm her. "You think recreating my home will make me forget what I've lost?" She let out a humourless chuckle. "This isn't home, Aldo. It's just a . . . photograph now. Not much different from this window."

"I know," he said softly, stepping closer. "But it's all I could do. Do you want me to get rid of it?"

She paused. "Not yet."

"Good. If you don't move in here, you can come anytime. The door will respond to your biometrics."

Selest turned away, staring at the curtains, the books and the pictures in the frames. Everything looked perfect, yet it felt hollow. "Did Dominic put you up to this? Is this some elaborate trick to make me fall in line?"

Aldo sighed. "No. This was my idea. I swear. Dominic doesn't care about your comfort, Selest. He cares about results. But I – I just wanted you to know you're not alone in this."

She clenched her jaw, torn between anger

and something she didn't want to name. "I am alone, Aldo. Abeni is dead. And you . . . You were part of that."

His face fell, and for a moment, he looked like the man she had once loved, burdened with the weight of his choices.

"I'm sorry," he said again, his voice barely above a whisper. "If I could go back, if I could change things . . . I would."

Selest closed her eyes, taking a deep breath. "You can't," she murmured before turning to face him. "And neither can I. But I'm here now. And I have work to do."

Aldo nodded slowly. "Then let me help, Lesty. Even if it's just . . . being here."

She studied him for a long moment. "Fine. But don't expect forgiveness and don't call me Lesty."

A small, sad smile touched his lips. "I won't."

Selest lingered for a moment longer

before stepping past him. "I'll see you around, Aldo."

He watched her go, the painful memories twisting them both. Selest didn't look back, but as she walked down the corridor, she couldn't shake the feeling that something within her had loosened. Whether it was for better or worse, she couldn't yet say.

7: Work

Selest woke slowly, her eyes adjusting to the dim light peeking through the curtains. The faint breath of filtered air mimicked the draught from an open window. For a moment, she allowed herself the illusion of home – imagining that the cooing of a turtle dove and the quiet hum of electric cars were real outside sounds and not coming from the alarm clock. The warmth of Aldo's body beside her was another familiar comfort she hadn't fully reconciled. His arm draped across her waist, his steady breathing grounding her. But the pain in her chest reappeared, saturated with the memories of yesterday and the days before.

She shifted slightly, her movement rousing Aldo. His eyes fluttered open, and he pulled her closer, his voice soft and groggy. "You're up early."

Selest turned to him, her lips quivering as she fought to contain her emotions.

"Aldo . . ." Her voice broke. She buried her face in his chest, tears spilling freely. "Another one . . . another poor child didn't make it yesterday."

Aldo's arms tightened around her, his brow furrowing. "I'm sorry, Lesty," he whispered. "This is tearing you apart."

She pulled back slightly, searching his eyes. "It's not just me, Aldo. It's all of us. These babies . . . they didn't consent to be part of this project."

He brushed a tear from her cheek. "You've done everything you could for them. No one else would have worked as tirelessly as you."

Selest shook her head. "But it's not enough, is it? Paul and I thought the new implants would integrate smoothly. We accounted for every variable, every potential rejection. And still . . . they're dying because of us. There's no sequence, no pattern. We can't even predict which organ will reject the integration next."

"You couldn't have foreseen this," Aldo said gently. "You're working under impossible pressure. Veir pushed this too fast – he's the one to blame, not you."

Selest sighed, staring at the ceiling. "It doesn't matter whose fault it is. Those babies were alive, Aldo. Breathing, crying, looking at us with trusting eyes. And then . . . they weren't. I don't want to feel what I am feeling now. I wish I could control it . . . switch it off or something."

"But you know better than anyone . . . feelings can't be controlled. We can only try to stop them from controlling us."

The silence stretched, suffocating. Aldo rubbed her back in slow, soothing circles, but it did little to calm the storm in her mind.

"What happens now?" he asked softly.

"Professor Sancho – I once knew her as a kind old woman, but she's changed. I want to suspend the implant trials to let the surviving children get stronger as they grow. She agreed but insisted we resume when they're eight months old. That's too soon. And Paul, ah! Paul is convinced we're close to a breakthrough. He doesn't want to stop at all."

Aldo studied her. "And what will you do?"

"I don't know," she admitted, voice thick with despair. "Part of me wants to discontinue completely. To say enough is enough. But what if Paul's right? Stopping now would mean everything we've done, everything we've lost, was for nothing."

Aldo cupped her face, his brow creased into a frown, so familiar but not stern this time. "Whatever you decide, Lesty, I'll support you. Be sure of that."

She gave him a sad smile of gratitude, but deep down, she knew no one could truly understand her torment, not even this beautiful man.

They had kept their relationship a secret for almost a year, just as they had Selest's reconstructed apartment. They both hoped that one day they would be free from this imprisonment and could start fresh. So, Selest left for work first that morning, slipping back to her assigned quarters to change into her lab clothes and water Lia, the lime tree that had grown a little taller.

Later, at the common breakfast, she and Aldo hardly exchanged glances, pretending they were strangers. He was leaving for a trade mission, promising to bring news from the outside world, their only glimpse beyond the facility's walls.

After breakfast, Selest checked on Fred in his lab before searching for Rokhel, who hadn't shown up at her workstation. She went to Sancho's office when she found no sign of Rokhel in the library or the sand garden. As she approached the observation area, voices from the adjoining room rose.

"You can't seriously be suggesting this, Professor!" Paul's tone was sharp with frustration.

"I am serious, Paul," Sancho replied, disturbingly calm. "This isn't about sentiment. It's about the project – the future of humanity. We cannot afford to let potential like this go to waste."

Selest hesitated, then stepped inside. Paul stood by a workstation, his expression torn between anger and desperation. Professor Sancho faced him, rigid and unyielding. Behind them, Rokhel sat silently on a stool.

"What's going on?" Selest asked.

Paul exhaled sharply. "You should hear this, Doctor. It's about Rokhel."

Selest turned. "What about her?"

Mel Sancho stepped forwards and said calmly, "Rokhel is pregnant. Approximately ten weeks. Paul is the father."

Selest blinked, momentarily stunned. She turned to Paul, whose flushed face betrayed his discomfort. "I see. And the problem?"

Rokhel spoke calmly. "I didn't plan for this, but I don't want to terminate the pregnancy. Paul and Professor Sancho disagree."

Sancho's expression remained resolute. "The foetus has undergone preliminary genetic testing. The results are promising – potentially invaluable. It could contribute significantly to the project as a subject or donor."

Selest's stomach twisted. "Professor!" she whispered. "You're talking about using Rokhel's baby . . . as a resource too? This child has parents."

"Science demands difficult choices," Sancho said coolly. "This child could save dozens of others. It's a logical decision."

Paul's voice trembled as he almost hissed at Sancho. "They wouldn't need saving if you didn't overdo the gene replacement. Now you need a subject with fresh stem cells and an uncompromised set of chromosomes." He sat down. "I can't do this, Selest. I can't work on my own kid. I won't."

Sancho's eyes were like ice. "You'll never know which one is yours, Paul. It will be placed with the others in the nursery once it's born with the next batch of subjects. Another number. Another asset."

Selest winced at these words and the unhealthy spark in the professor's cold eyes. She turned to Rokhel. "And you? What do *you* want?"

Rokhel hesitated, gripping her abdomen. "I thought I could leave and take the baby to my parents. Surely, Veir would let me go in my condition. But if this baby could help the project . . . maybe it's worth it. Not as a subject, but later. As a cell donor."

Selest stared at her, horrified. "You're talking about using your child's body for this. How can you even consider it?"

Paul turned to Selest, his voice breaking. "Please, Selest. I can't let this happen. You're the only one I trust to terminate this . . . problem forever. This old crow will steal and clone my baby."

Selest stepped back, shaking her head. "No. This is more than I can take. I won't be part of this. You're all insane!"

She turned and walked out, her heart pounding.

Her steps were firm as she approached Dominic Veir's private quarters, a place shrouded in secrecy. A guard escorted her to Dominic's study. The man himself was seated behind a sleek black desk, his posture relaxed but commanding. She had not seen him for months and had almost forgotten his appearance. Dominic Veir carried his fifty years with an effortless authority. His brown hair, streaked with silver at the temples, was combed back precisely. His grey eyes, harder with time, dissected rather than observed. He dressed with the same meticulousness – an immaculate suit, not a thread out of place. No jewellery, no excess. Just control. He didn't hunt; he *collected*.

And once something was in his grasp, he never let it go.

The room was nothing like she had imagined – it was some kind of grotesque museum.

She stopped in her tracks, her breath catching. Shelves lined the walls, not with books but with glass jars, each containing something twisted, incomplete. Some were no bigger than malformed dolls. Others bore evidence of Paul's early experiments – wires and devices encased in translucent plastic and embedded in skulls, spines and the crude architecture of forced evolution.

She recognised some of them. Subjects she had worked on. Lives she had tried to forget.

Dominic rose, watching her reaction with sharp amusement. "Grim, isn't it?" His tone was casual, as if remarking on the weather.

Selest couldn't answer. Her throat had gone dry, and a suffocating regret pressed against her ribs.

"They are necessary reminders." He stepped to one of the jars, tapping the glass lightly. "Failures teach us more than successes ever could."

Selest forced her voice out, barely above a whisper. "These were children ... people! How can you keep them like this?"

"They were not people," Dominic corrected coldly. "They were attempts. Prototypes. Their genes were meddled with, and their uniqueness was diluted by multiple cloning. They never had time to become anything else. But each brought us closer to perfection. Would you rather they be forgotten entirely?"

She looked away, fists clenched. "You could have cremated them like the others. Given them some dignity."

"And waste the opportunity to learn?" He raised an eyebrow. "You disappoint me, Selest. I thought you, of all people, would understand by now."

She met his eyes. "Understand what? That you squeeze everything dry, just in case it will serve your special goal? That you refuse to let go of even this?"

"Sentimentality is a weakness," he said in a voice like steel.

She opened her mouth to argue but stopped when he turned to another jar holding a tiny, barely formed thing.

His tone shifted. "Did you notice that genetically identical clones can have vastly different rejection rates for implants? Same DNA, yet the body's response varies wildly. The key lies in cellular development – environment, stressors . . ."

He spoke for a full five minutes. Against her will, Selest felt herself pulled in. Instinct overrode revulsion, and reason drowned out horror. Soon they were debating rejection rates and material compatibility. She proposed carbon and silicon polymers; he raised concerns about structural stability. Before she knew it, their ideas had drifted somewhere worse – beyond technology and genetic engineering, into the realm of biological transplantation.

For a moment she forgot the jars, caught in the rhythm of problem-solving. But when she remembered, she broke the trance, clamping her hands over her ears. The silence that followed was long and corrosive.

Then Dominic leaned back against his desk, arms folded. His eyes cut through her thoughts. "You didn't come here to discuss translimination, did you?"

In a painful wave, reality came rushing back. "It's about Rokhel," she admitted.

A flicker of interest. "Ah, the young engineer. What about her?"

"She's pregnant with Paul's child. I'm here to ask that you allow her to raise the baby with her family's support. I'm sure you can come up with a convincing story about how she survived the blast. You've proven yourself creative in matters like that."

Dominic sighed, shaking his head like a disappointed mentor. "Oh, that. I already know. Paul should have stuck to the kitchen girls – mixing work with personal matters was reckless."

Selest pressed on. "Sancho wants to keep the baby for the project. But Rokhel wants to leave and be a mother. I'm asking you to let her go."

Dominic's lips curled into a faint smirk. "And Paul? Let me guess – too morally conflicted? Really?"

She frowned. "He wants me to terminate it and free him from responsibility. But that should be Rokhel's decision to make."

Dominic considered her words, then said, "If Rokhel wants to leave, she can. But the baby stays."

Selest stared at him. "You can't be serious. She isn't livestock. She never agreed to this, not like Suli—"

"She's an employee," he cut in. "One who also signed a contract, knowing the stakes. She can walk away as she came except for the full purse and her new story. But the child belongs to the project. Non-negotiable. Don't concern yourself with her feelings. I'll pay her enough to forget all this."

Selest felt cold from despair and helplessness – the cruel finality of it. She wanted to argue, but what was the point? Dominic Veir always got what he wanted.

He leaned in, his voice deliberate. "You came here for Rokhel. My decision makes her choose her sacrifice. And it is final."

Selest turned and walked out.

8: Time

The next few years were devoid of joy and ease, though there had never been much of either to begin with. Selest had not been entirely surprised when Rokhel decided to stay. The good woman refused the money. When the time came, to Sancho's great displeasure, both Paul and Selest were present at the birth. Rokhel had held her son with trembling, sweaty hands and whispered that she had no regrets. She had made her decision partially because of Selest's unwavering stance when she first learned of the pregnancy. But also because of the news seeping in from the outside world.

Something was happening outside the resort. Something vast, incomprehensible.

For a long time, humanity felt that only the name of the glorious Platinum Age remained. Now, long in decline, its leftovers were crumbling before their eyes. For centuries, scientists, inventors and makers of all arts ruled as the elite, the architects of civilisation's progress and the guiding force of humanity's expansion into the unknown. It had been an era of great ambition that held the promise of reason above all else. But promises were fragile things, effortlessly twisted and easily shattered.

Religious sects, once fringe movements, had erupted into dominance across every region. Their influence spread like wildfire, fuelled by discontent, fear and a growing distrust of those who had once been revered. The Platinum Age, they declared, had been nothing more than a mirage – a grand deception, a lie spun by the intellectual elite to hoard power and wealth. The great projects of the past, the very ones that had shaped human progress, were rebranded as grotesque betrayals.

One particular story was fervently seized upon: the famous KOSI Colonisation Project, which started from Jupiter's orbital stations. Kepler's Object of Special Interest.

Several pairs of ships were launched towards the constellation Lyra more than three hundred years ago, starting in the year 3000, aiming at a distant world orbiting a red dwarf.

It had been humanity's most ambitious interstellar endeavour to secure a future among the stars. But now the narrative had shifted. Although no one expected to hear any reports from the colonists soon, the time that passed should have had some bright indication of success. The expedition, the preachers claimed, had been nothing but a farce – a monumental act of corruption, a crime against God. Those ships had never been meant to succeed. The leaders of the Platinum Age had stolen unfathomable sums, sending innocent colonists to their deaths in the cold abyss of space.

And that was only the beginning.

It was not enough to discredit the scientists; they had to be condemned. Faith was the true path, the only path. Those who had spent their lives shaping reality through logic and discovery were cast as heretics, their work painted as arrogance, their unbelief the gravest of sins. The Platinum Age had defied the divine; now the reckoning had come.

Punishment, the preachers roared, was inevitable.

Selest had swotted every scrap of information she could find. Reports from the outside were scarce, censored and distorted by layers of propaganda. Yet the patterns were clear. Books were being burned, just like during the dark times. Universities ransacked. Scientists, philosophers and other great minds executed. Cities that had once been centres of knowledge and research were falling to mobs, to zealots who saw laboratories as temples of blasphemy. Scientists were disappearing – some fled, some silenced. A few turned, renouncing their past and kneeling before the new order. What had been a slow, gradual process over the last three hundred years suddenly sped up into a terrifying rush.

And within the isolated walls of their secretive compound, Selest watched as the world she had once known slipped further and further into the past. Although they couldn't see much of what was happening outside, they felt some effect. Life in Ozhogino had not been so luxurious lately. It was becoming increasingly difficult for the resort owner to buy delicacies and quality clothing for his residents. Priority was given to necessary materials and medicines.

One day, Aldo leaned back in his chair, watching Selest with open curiosity. "So, what *did* happen to the Platinum Age?" he asked. "I was never much for history, but lately, it seems like the only thing worth cramming."

Selest sighed, rubbing her temples. "Today it's generally accepted that it ended in 3241. KOSI people thought that getting the first message from the colony would restore their faith in the scheme. Instead, society called it a hoax – just another way to keep them in line."

Aldo frowned. "That's ridiculous."

She gave a wry smile. "Not really. By then, most people had checked out. Life was too good. They had everything – comfort, pleasure, health, endless opportunities. The ones who actually *did* things, the ones who pushed the world forwards became fewer and fewer. Meanwhile, the rest just . . . enjoyed themselves.

Brought up families, relished art and played sports. But it wasn't enough. When people lose a greater purpose in their lives, they stop growing and start seeking easier ways to feel worthy. Even if it is just a feeling."

She paused, choosing her words. "Then came the pushback. Some people started rejecting the whole system. First, it was just hobby clubs and groups with common interests – nature lovers, history buffs, those who study the occult. Then someone – no one even knows who – said the word *God* out loud, and it all spiralled from there."

Aldo raised a brow. "And now?"

Selest shrugged. "Now the real scientists work underground, decoding KOSI messages from the colony every thirty years. Even the international academies barely acknowledge it – too many scandals."

She stood, stretching. "Come with me to see Rokhel? She knows we're together."

Aldo was already pulling her into his arms, stopping her in the doorway with a kiss.

"I think everyone knows, Lesty," he murmured. "Or at least, they *suspect*."

Selest smirked. "Let them suspect a little longer then."

Selest had not visited Rokhel in some time. The passing years had drawn them into separate routines, each deeply immersed in their own work and battles. But she had always made time to check on little Gleb when she could. And now, as she walked towards Rokhel's quarters, she braced for a visit to the Common Nursery; a visit she had committed to but wasn't sure about.

She knocked once before stepping inside. Rokhel sat cross-legged on the floor, Gleb nestled in her lap, a squidgy blue ball clutched in his tiny hands.

"You came," Rokhel said simply. Her tone carried no real surprise but a quiet observation. "Despite your worries."

"Of course. It's his third birthday. I also brought a gift and wanted to see how you both are. Here! I think Gleb is ready to meet little Ziggy." And she pulled her ginger cat from her pocket.

Gleb dropped the ball he was holding and raised both hands towards the soft toy. He looked up at Selest and grinned, his bright eyes full of life.

"Zizzie!" he said enthusiastically.

Rokhel glanced at her son with a rather sad expression. "He's fine. Sancho still doesn't ask much of him. A few blood and tissue samples, but nothing else. I think Paul put his foot down."

Selest exhaled, relieved. "And you?"

Rokhel hesitated. "Paul and I . . . we've found a way to make it work. Maybe it's because Gleb's growing. Maybe it's because we're both clinging to something human in all this madness. But we're stronger than we were before."

Selest studied her, searching for any sign of repentance. She found none. Instead, there was something close to contentment, however fragile. "I'm glad."

Gleb wriggled in Rokhel's arms, reaching towards Selest. She lifted him, acknowledged that he was getting heavy and settled him against her hip. He was warm, solid, real. It was a quiet comfort she had not expected.

"Shall we go to the nursery?" Rokhel asked. "The little ones are waiting."

Seles tensed but then exhaled with determination. "Sure, let's do it."

They made their way through the corridors, arriving at the nursery where the youngest subjects were cared for. The moment they stepped inside, Selest faced them – the small Loaders, indistinguishable from ordinary children at first glance but unmistakable upon closer inspection. Their movements were too precise, their awareness too sharp. And yet, they played just as children should, laughing, chasing, existing in the brief innocence of childhood. Seeing them here, nestled among cushions and toys on the carpet, felt strange. Selest always avoided this. On the operating table, under anaesthesia, they were something else entirely – clinical, distant. She barely saw them, even in the recovery room, under the nurses' care. By then, it was Paul who evaluated the results, measuring success, so she met them in data rather than faces.

Beneath a huge lamp simulating the warmth of a summer afternoon, there was a large playground filled with objects for entertainment. A large carpet dyed the almost-forgotten shade of real grass lay clean. Birdsong intertwined with soft music from hidden speakers created a gentle, soothing atmosphere. Four women in uniform moved among the children, reading from brightly illustrated sheets, guiding their play and maintaining order.

Rokhel joined the nannies, her movements fluid and familiar, as she showed her son the new toys. Her voice softened, blending with the gentle hum of the room, while the boy's curious hands reached out, eager to explore. The other children glanced at him with fleeting, indifferent looks, their expressions distant, as if instinctively sensing he was not one of them – not as advanced and much weaker. Then, just as quickly, they returned to their activities, their minds already pulled elsewhere, leaving him unnoticed amid the room's bright colours.

Only one girl, a couple of years older, with copper curls that caught the artificial sunlight, drifted closer. She studied Gleb with quiet curiosity, her regard steady and assessing. When he shyly offered her a toy, she accepted it with the patience of a grown-up, her small fingers brushing his in a gesture that felt almost ceremonial, as if she alone had granted him a place, however temporary, in their strange little world.

The room's corners were shadowed, with soft chairs and low tables set with snacks and drinks. Dominic was there, watching with an assessing and, strangely, almost caring expression.

He turned to Selest, who sat in the chair next to him. "Forty-seven," Dominic murmured. "Forty-seven unique individuals – almost a population, a new race."

Selest felt the old loathing for him stir. "Forty-seven out of several hundred. Maybe count how many never made it to this day. They're only three to five years old, and I'm just relieved we've run out of that stupid loser's eggs. Did you come to admire the result of your evil? Are they still just numbers to you? I bet you don't even know they've given themselves names. Do you know all forty-seven? What's the name of the red-headed girl?"

Dominic smirked. "First of all, there are more than forty-seven if you count how many siblings they're stitched together from. And second, if I wanted more material, I could get it. I have a good reason to pause for now. After the last earthquake in Canada in '52, the mystics nearly uncovered a second resort. Ours is underground because of the climate. The others aren't. Still, it's becoming too risky. I want to stop now and focus on the development of what we have."

Selest grimaced. "You're disgusting. I hate you."

"Yes, yes, I know." His chuckle was infuriating. "But you love your work. You care for those Loaders as if they were your own children. You love them, you pity them . . . Shame you don't feel the same about the very first Loader. We have forty-seven here, but only one survived from the first attempt half a century ago. Me."

She froze. "You?"

His expression didn't change. "The first Loader that everyone heard about. The one who saved the Institute for the Study of Artificial Black Holes and built entire residential complexes atop giant trees in dust-storm districts." He tilted his head. "Why do you think I always believed in our success? Especially after you came up with those transmitters in synthetic ribs and nail cords. Not a single one's been rejected yet."

"Why didn't you ever —"

"Because it would've exposed the source of my wealth. I'd have lost business partners for not being careful enough in the past. Better people think I'm just a genius with incredible luck." His voice was calm, almost amused. "Now you know. Though honestly? My survival was probably just a fluke."

Selest remained speechless.

"I am not a monster, Selest. None of us are. We are preserving something greater than ourselves. I have brought more minds into Eternum, and there are others – other projects, resorts, space stations and the Mars colony – all still carrying the torch of the Platinum Age. We are not alone here."

For the first time in a long while, Selest felt something other than dread. It was not hope. Not yet. But perhaps he was right, and this was the only way.

"Karagoz."

"What?" Selest snapped from her thoughts.

"The redhead. Her name is Karagoz," Dominic repeated.

9: Gleb

Five more years passed. Time in this place seemed to stretch and fold in on itself, marked not by seasons but by research milestones and the steady march of scientific necessity. For Selest, those years were considerably lighter than the ones before. The screams of newborns had faded into memory – Eternum had simply run out of frozen zygotes. There were no more tiny subjects to cut open, no fresh lives to mar in pursuit of perfection. Her work with Paul had become infrequent, reduced to sporadic consultations as he meticulously collected data on the mental and physical development of the young Loaders. Instead, since Rokhel became a mother, Selest often found herself in Rokhel's former position beside Fred Shademaker, immersed in refining bio-suits – living second skins designed to grow with the children, adapting seamlessly to their evolving bodies.

The laboratory was filled with the soft whirring of machines and the faint scent of sterilised metal. Selest stood in front of the observation panel, letting the bio-suit settle over her skin like a second layer of muscle and skin. The light-grey fabric clung to her from her feet to her neck, its surface rippling as it adjusted to her form. Almost liquid in texture, the material moved with an eerie sentience, shifting ever so slightly as if breathing in sync with her body.

Silver threads embroidered the suit in a pattern resembling blood vessels, glimmering under the cold laboratory lights. They weren't merely decorative. These fine, glistening filaments were an intricate fusion of tubes and micro-wires, winding like a circulatory and nervous system across Selest's limbs and torso. Beneath the surface, they pulsed with invisible activity, controlled by the suit's homeostatic intelligence, monitoring every function of her body. Selest flexed her fingers, and the fabric followed seamlessly, contracting and releasing like a living organism, responding with microscopic precision to every movement she made, doubling her strength.

Shademaker watched from behind a console, his eyes darting between the data scrolling across the screen and Selest herself.

"Try a deep breath," he instructed.

She complied, inhaling slowly. The suit tightened around her ribcage for a split second before easing again, mimicking the expansion and contraction of the intercostal muscles. A safety measure: if the wearer stopped breathing, the suit could replicate thoracic movement, forcing air into unresponsive lungs to keep oxygen circulating. Selest exhaled, the suit flexing in tandem.

"Good," Fred murmured. "Now let's see if it picks up on a sudden drop in vitals."

She heard a faint chime as Fred activated the test sequence. Immediately, the fabric along her spine tensed, ready to engage if necessary. If her heart faltered, the suit's AI could override natural processes and restart it with an electric pulse, flooding her system with emergency stabilisation compounds stored in microscopic reservoirs.

However, as long as the host remained conscious, their neurowear implant granted them limited control. Selest concentrated, sending a mental command through the interface embedded at the base of her skull. The suit responded instantly, altering the material's rigidity around her knees and elbows, reinforcing her stance. She flexed her fingers again, this time willing the suit to slightly increase its support around her wrists – an adaptation designed for fine motor control under strenuous conditions.

Fred clapped his hands together. "Brilliant. It's working exactly as intended."

Selest turned her head, feeling the suit adjust fluidly, like a living thing wrapped around her body. "It's remarkable, Genatsvale," she admitted, running her hands over the shimmering silver threads.

Ever the insufferable genius, Fred admired his brilliance aloud as they adjusted the microfilament matrices within the synthetic tendons of a prototype.

"If a child loses a finger," Fred said, tapping on the interface with a gleam in his eye, "the suit will form a glove with a synthetic prosthesis. Phenomenal. Someday we'll manage this for an entire arm or leg. For now, just fingers and feet. Oh, I am good! I am so good!"

Selest barely acknowledged his enthusiasm, wondering that science had already reshaped life itself – who was to say where it would stop? Could these new social movements stop it? But before she could decide, the lab door burst open. Rokhel stood there, her face pale, eyes wide with an anxiety that pierced the sterile calm.

"Come quickly," Rokhel gasped, her voice thin with fear. "It's Gleb."

Without a word, Selest quickly but reluctantly changed, and they followed her through the labyrinthine corridors to the classroom, where the other children sat in silent rows, eyes fixed on their computer screens. The glow of holographic projections painted their young faces in cold blues and greens. But all Selest saw was Gleb, crumpled on the floor, his small frame trembling slightly, his eyes wide and disoriented.

Paul and Mel Sancho were already there, crouched beside him. Paul's face was drawn, his hands hovering uncertainly as if afraid to touch his son. Sancho, ever cold, scrolled through data on a nearby console, her brow furrowed in frustration.

"He just fell," Rokhel whispered, kneeling beside her son. "He couldn't remember his password for the school programme, and then . . . just fell."

Paul glanced at Selest, his expression pleading. She swallowed the lump rising in her throat and kneeled to meet Gleb's unfocused eyes. His lips trembled, but no words came.

"I can't make a diagnosis without more tests," Sancho muttered, her fingers flying over the data logs. She frowned deeper, scrolling through Gleb's medical records. Just then, a shadow moved beside her. Karagoz, now ten, stepped forwards, her copper curls gleaming under the artificial light. She peered at the screen, her expression calm and eerily mature.

But Sancho barely acknowledged her, her frustration mounting. "The initial genetic tests didn't reveal any problems. Perhaps the mutation arose later."

Paul shook his head vehemently. "No. You missed something. Or you hid it."

Before Sancho could respond, Karagoz spoke softly, her voice cutting through the tension like a scalpel.

"He's got something called Progressive Synaptic Dissociation Syndrome."

The room fell into stunned silence. Karagoz crouched beside Rokhel, her sharp eyes reflecting knowledge far beyond her years.

"It's not an infection or a fever. It's in Gleb's genes – buried there since birth, waiting. His brain's losing connections, like threads snapping one by one. That's why he fell. His body forgot how to stand, even for a second. And the memory loss? That's the synapses in his hippocampus breaking apart. It's like someone's tearing pages out of a book, and you can't get them back."

Rokhel's face crumpled, denial rising like a fragile shield. "But there's a cure, right?"

Karagoz looked at Gleb. "Not yet. Maybe someday. But not soon enough."

Paul squeezed his eyes shut, his hand clenched into a fist. Rokhel sat Gleb up and hugged him, her tears falling silently onto his tousled hair.

Sancho was the first to break the stillness. "There is one option," she said quietly, clinical detachment settling back over her face like a mask. "We can save him – but only if we turn him into a Loader."

Selest felt the words like a blow, her heart recoiling. She met Rokhel's tear-filled eyes and then Paul's haunted look, knowing the battle that would come next. She knew, too, that hope always came at a terrible price in this place. All this time, Fred Shademaker stood silently next to Selest at a loss for words.

Sancho looked at them in turn, indifferent to the mounting tension. "Well? You heard the girl."

Paul's face twisted with rage. "I heard her," he snapped, stepping forwards with clenched fists. "A ten-year-old Loader knows more than you, is that it? Or did you hide the PSDS from us, knowing this was how you'd get him on the operating table?"

Sancho didn't flinch, didn't even blink. The silence started to suffocate the whole room.

Selest broke it, her voice low and deliberate. "Mel, you ran the test for the SYNP1 mutation soon after Gleb was born. The result is recorded as inconclusive." She pointed at the screen, her finger trembling slightly. "Deliberate or not, that fact doesn't change. But Mel . . ." Selest turned to Sancho, her eyes sharp. "We could have corrected it in the early stages.

I could have synthesised a drug."

Rokhel sobbed, the weeping brittle like glass cracking under pressure. "He was a bit wobbly before. Mel said it was normal and that living underground can be disorienting for a child. She said it was nothing."

Selest's face hardened. "I guess it's too late now." She exhaled, the breath seeming saturated with regret. "Now we must adapt Loader brain implants to compensate for lost motor functions and memory gaps. Gleb will have to become a Loader. I am sorry, Paul ... Rokhel."

Paul's body tensed like a coiled spring. His rage boiled over as he stormed towards Sancho, stopping an inch from her face. His breath was ragged, his fists trembling at his sides. "Don't you ever come near my son again," he hissed.

Sancho stood her ground, her expression unreadable.

The room became silent again, broken only by Rokhel's quiet sobbing. Selest turned away, unable to bear the sight of Paul's devastation, and fixed her scrutiny on Mel Sancho, still grappling with the disbelief of such a cruel choice.

Sancho stood there, unbothered, her expression disturbingly serene. Then she gave Fred Shademaker a small, careless shrug and a soft, almost whimsical giggle. "Those Loaders. Aren't they great? They even frighten me sometimes with what they can do."

Old Fred recoiled in horror.

Selest stepped closer, her breath sharp in her chest, heat flaring in her hands as if her shock had turned into a fever. Sancho was smiling – empty, brittle lips curved under watery eyes. And in that moment, with crystal clarity, Selest saw what had always been hidden beneath the facade: the old woman wasn't indifferent. She was utterly mad.

10: Home

Selest had been in the resort for so long – almost thirteen years – it had begun to feel like the only world left. The relationship between Aldo and Selest was no longer a secret to anyone, nor was their shared apartment, where she had moved permanently, bringing Lia, the lime tree, with her. The outside had become a distant, crumbling memory, a ghost of a past that no longer seemed real. Yet, one day, everything changed again. Dominic Veir, ever calculating and cautious, finally trusted her enough to let her leave the resort, although briefly. It was a rare privilege and one that delighted Aldo beyond words.

She joined Aldo and his team on their two- or three-day supply runs to North American and European states and cities. They gathered essential goods, fulfilled project orders and exchanged updates with other resistance groups. On one of those trips, which led them close to her home town, Selest made a request Aldo was not thrilled about: she wanted to visit her old flat block.

"Lesty, you know that's a bad idea. You're supposed to be dead. It's for your own protection. All your things were recovered and moved to the resort ages ago. There's nothing left for you there. Last time I collected something for you, everyone there was fine."

"But that was years ago. I had neighbours I care about," she insisted. "I need to know if my friends are okay."

He sighed heavily, rubbing his temple.

"Fine. But keep your mask on, and be quick about it. One hour. I'll wait for you at the old car park nearby. We can't linger long – the thermocopter can only touch down briefly before we risk an attack from the mystics."

When they landed, he walked with her to the building and gave her a passionate, lingering kiss before turning back to his vessel. She walked towards the familiar door with a dizzy head and a smile hidden beneath her dust mask.

The sight of her old neighbourhood was more shocking than she had anticipated. The once-familiar flat block was almost unrecognisable. The ground-floor windows were smashed and boarded up, a weak defence against the relentless sandstorms. Sand and debris piled in every corner. The vibrant birds, flowers and dwarf trees that had once brought life to the indoor square were long gone. The fountains were dry, their basins cracked and empty. Once a bustling centre of trade, music and laughter, the market hall was now a hollow shell.

Aunt Tessie's – the place she had loved most – stood desolate. The plastic chairs, once neatly arranged for customers, now encircled a rough makeshift brazier. Someone had burned all the wooden furniture for warmth. Smoke still curled lazily from smouldering table legs. Someone had been here recently. People still lived here.

"Hey, you . . ." a sharp but familiar voice called from behind the counter. "Unless you've got food to share, get out. We don't take in strangers."

Selest turned, her heart skipping.

"Tessie?" she exclaimed, removing her mask before remembering all the precautions.

The woman before her was gaunt, her once-plump frame reduced by hardship, but there was no mistaking her. Tessie's sharp eyes narrowed, then widened with recognition. She hesitated momentarily, then called off the others who had begun to circle Selest warily.

"Selest?" Tessie smiled the usual smile she had for her favourite customers. "Finally! You're back."

One of the men darted up the stairs before Selest could question it. She was overwhelmed with emotion, embracing the people she had once known. Yet, as they talked, one revelation unsettled her more than anything else: they already knew she wasn't dead.

"How?" she demanded. "Who told you?"

Tessie hesitated before answering. "Your old friend, Maria. She moved into your old flat recently. She said you'd come back any day now."

Selest frowned. "Maria? I don't remember any Maria."

A moment later, a figure descended the staircase. When the woman in a dark-blue coat stepped into the light, Selest gasped, her breath catching in her throat.

"Abeni?" The name tumbled from her lips in disbelief. "My word . . . you're alive!"

Abeni smiled, a knowing, almost serene expression on her face. "Looks like we both are. And I've been waiting for you."

It was her, indeed. Slimmer, older. And instead of the shiny golden mane – twisted black curls. Their reunion was overwhelming. They embraced and went together to the flat that used to be Selest's. Now it was refurnished with simple plastic furniture, made more for a patio than an apartment. Abeni's story was both miraculous and terrifying. Michael – another name Selest had long buried – had returned to the tundra for Abeni soon after Selest was taken away. His electric track was very fast; he had driven her south to the safety of the nearest town and ensured she received medical help.

"He was sure that you had left me to die," Abeni admitted. "But I never held it against you. I told you to save yourself. You did what I wanted."

Relief flooded Selest, but it was short-lived.

As Abeni continued her tale, the joy of their reunion darkened. Selest listened, unease growing with every word. The friend she had known – the passionate scientist, the fierce advocate for reason – had changed. In her place stood a woman filled with conviction of another kind entirely. She had changed her name. She was now the leader of a new organisation: the Cruisers.

"I had my spies in every trade point Michael told me about. As soon as you were seen at one of them, I knew you wouldn't resist coming here one day. I want you by my side again, Sel. You know better than anyone else that the Loaders are unnatural," Abeni said, her voice passionate, fervent. "You told me so yourself. What they do to those children, the experiments, the modifications . . . it's wrong. Unethical. You and I rebelled against it, against Dominic and his Eternum. We were meant to use our knowledge for something greater."

Selest's stomach turned. "And what would that be?"

Abeni's eyes shone. "To guide humanity back to its true path. To evacuate the faithful and place them in the hands of the Lord. He will care for us, as he always has."

Selest took a step back. She knew that look – the dangerous certainty, the unwavering belief. The story was getting worse with every word.

Michael had told Abeni that despite her deception – spending the night with him only to steal the electronic key to the elevator – he had still managed to convince Dominic to send her to another resort. Selest came to realise that Dominic had known about the young women's escape plan all along. Still, Dominic hadn't expected such dexterity or speed. He had weighed his options and decided that while Selest needed to be taught a lesson, Abeni didn't have to die. Still, it would serve his objectives better if Selest bore the full burden of the failure alone.

Michael left Ozhogino, never to return, and took Abeni to an underground medical centre in the nearest city. The mystics, despite their relentless hunt for scientists, had thus far left the medics alone, as they did not place their faith in godly entities when it came to their own health. Abeni was saved. The young woman's recovery was swift, and when she and Michael were forced to leave the centre and wander, she became his lover.

Their plan had been simple: Michael was to meet one of Dominic's men, who would take them to the Canadian Resort of Hope. But the contact never showed. Only much later did they learn of the earthquake that had obliterated the safe zone in that region. Stranded, they decided to seek out the Resistance themselves.

A few years ago, some types of public transport still functioned, including a high-speed train across the Diomede Bridge. Michael sold his track and managed to pay for the journey all the way to Edmonton. Knowing the trade routes well, he led Abeni from one exchange point to another. They scavenged through abandoned houses, stole supplies where they could, and spent nights huddled in ruins, hoping to stumble upon the right people. Instead, the wrong ones found them first.

In the trading post of Montana, a group of men clad in monklike robes ambushed them at a derelict checkpoint. They were overpowered, beaten and stripped of their belongings. When they woke, they found themselves locked in a cold, damp basement, the scent of rot thick in the air. Soon after, a man descended the steps to greet them. He was young, tall and strikingly handsome, his robes pristine despite the decay around him. A massive golden cross hung from his neck, most likely stolen from a museum. He called himself Father Sebastian.

He was a preacher, he told them, a man of faith who had found his calling in these desperate times. At first, Abeni spat in his face, but Father Sebastian was patient. He visited the basement often, speaking of the world's decay, the sin that had led humanity to its downfall, and the salvation he alone could offer. His voice had power, a certainty that made doubt feel like an affliction.

Michael refused to succumb. Abeni watched him change as her scepticism eroded under the weight of the preacher's words. They beat him relentlessly, mercilessly, until he no longer had the strength to argue, but he never yielded. Instead his eyes shifted, its warmth fading, replaced by something colder – disappointment. Contempt.

When Father Sebastian approached her one evening and asked if she wished to be saved, she agreed.

That night, she and Michael were injected with a special medicine and brought before Father Sebastian. He stood up to his waist in a great basin of clean water and beckoned her forwards. "Look at what they have done to the world," he told her. "Look at what they have done to you and to this man. Your bright mind and talent were meant for more. The Lord saved you from death in the cold desert for a reason. He has a plan for you, as he has for all of us. All you must do is accept his love. I am willing to pass it to you," he said.

Abeni's voice took on a fervent, almost hypnotic rhythm as she spoke, her eyes alight with something Selest couldn't quite recognise – devotion, madness or both.

"You see, Sel, my heart resisted at first. Just like yours is now. Just like I used to resist – so sure of my intelligence and righteousness. But suffering is a teacher like no other, and I have learned." She leaned closer, lowering her voice as if sharing a secret. "Michael chose to remain blind. He closed his heart, and his life was offered to the Lord so his soul could be saved. But I . . . I began to see. Before, I also thought I knew better – science, logic, all that nonsense we clung to. But what did it give us? Pain, war, death. And I nearly perished holding onto it."

She straightened, exhaling slowly as if savouring the memory. "But the Lord had other plans. Father Sebastian – what a beautiful man he is – showed me. He asked me, 'Do you wish to save humanity from sin, death, Judgement Day when the sun will burst and burn away the filth of this world?' And, Sel, I knew then – everything we had done before was meaningless. All our so-called knowledge, all our sterile ambitions. The only path was his path. The only salvation was through him."

Selest stayed silent, watching as Abeni – Maria – smiled softly, almost dreamily. "I had to relinquish my man, my past, my body, my name and my burdens to earn forgiveness."

Her gaze sharpened, fixing Selest with an intensity that made her stomach twist as she described how she had stepped into the font, naked, before Father Sebastian, holy water chilling her skin. And when his hands found her body, it was not only in benediction but in something deeper, something that sent a shudder through her. For a fleeting moment, something felt off – but then she surrendered, convincing herself that his touch, whether reverent or possessive, was merely devotion to the godly cause. "Let me show you the path to divine bliss," he whispered. And she accepted. The warmth that followed, the euphoria, the absolute certainty that she had found her truth – it was overwhelming.

"I agreed to the holy sacrifice and spilled Michael's blood into that font myself; with his life, I poured out everything I was before. I let Sebastian and the reddened holy water take me, let them cleanse me, let them wash away the corruption of my old life. He blessed me and gave me divine joy, and at that moment, I understood. I saw the Lord. I was reborn. And now I stand with my brothers and sisters, the chosen ones, and I will guide the worthy to salvation. We will not let the self-important progressors of humanity interfere in God's design. Only he will decide who is saved. Not science. Not living machines."

She had shed her past like a serpent's skin. She had dived into the baptismal font, denouncing the girl she had been. When she rose, she was no longer Abeni. She was Sister Maria.

This very different woman with Abeni's sweet face leaned in, her breath warm against Selest's cheek. The scent of incense clung to her robes, sharp and cloying. Her voice, barely above a whisper, carried an unbearable certainty. "You can still be saved. You can still be free of all this. Come with me. Let me help you. Let me show you the way."

Selest forced herself to breathe, to steady the pounding in her chest. This wasn't Abeni. Abeni had been sharp, defiant and full of quiet mirth, even in the darkest moments. This woman was a stranger wrapped in her skin, her voice tainted with something far worse than certainty – fanaticism.

From the day of her initiation and in the following years, Sister Maria walked beside Father Sebastian as his devoted disciple and, eventually, as his equal. She gathered followers and preached his gospel with fire in her voice. Maria conceived the idea of the Cruisers, named after the celestial journey they would take to salvation.

Now they all wore their navy- and sky-blue robes with pride, a symbol of the endless heavens they would one day traverse. The plan was simple: humanity was corrupt beyond redemption. Technology had been its downfall, so technology would become its salvation – but only under the hand of God. Not the false prophets of progress, not the scientists who played with life and death like children with toys. It would be Sister Maria and her faithful who would see it done.

"I have to go," Selest said firmly.

Maria smiled. "You're not leaving. I still love you, Sel. I have found you and will never lose you again."

A distant explosion rocked the ground beneath them. Selest's head snapped towards the square.

"What was that?" she demanded.

Maria's voice was calm, almost soothing. "The thermocopter. It was attacked. It self-destructed, as you knew it would. I made sure there would be no survivors."

Selest's blood turned to ice. The world's edges blurred as if the ground itself had fallen beneath her. The breath left her lungs, and for one terrifying moment, she wasn't sure if she could take another. Abeni was truly gone. Her means of return was gone. Aldo was gone. And she was trapped once again.

11: Maria

"Of course, I heard every word. I understood your story in all its clarity . . . Sister Maria!"

Selest spat the name like a curse, something that had no place in the world of reason, her voice sharp enough to cut. Even the air seemed to still.

"You let yourself be seduced," she continued, steady and cold. "Mind ruined by a charming fraud, a master manipulator who broke you in that basement. He wore you down when you were already exhausted from the road. I can see it. He whispered sweet, poisonous things, drugged you, fucked you in a bathtub, and fed you poetic nonsense about fate and salvation. And to buy your loyalty, he made you kill Michael. Because nothing cements conviction like blood on your hands. Potential future blood, too, as you betrayed the secrets of the Eternum Project and its location to the sect. And now" – she leaned forwards, her voice like iron – "if you ever sober up and let reason in, the guilt will devour you whole, unless you use that suicide pill of yours. Do you still carry it? You will take it eventually when you mess things up completely. You know it. So what do you do when you lose? You double down. Convince yourself that it was justified and righteous and had to be done. Because the alternative – the truth – is unbearable now. You will keep killing for some time, as it's only getting easier."

Her voice dropped to a near-whisper. "Do you even know what they injected you with back then?"

Maria's hand flew across Selest's face before she even seemed aware of it. A sharp crack filled the room. Selest staggered back, her skin burning. Maria winced, shaking out her hand as though the force of the slap had hurt her just as much.

"Bliss!" she snarled, raw with frustration and triumph. She shot to her feet, sending her chair clattering to the ground. "It was Bliss, a divine compound that opens the inner eye and lets you see beyond the veil into another dimension."

Selest pressed a hand to her stinging cheek, a slow, mirthless laugh escaping her lips. It held no joy, only astonishment. "And these," Selest said, "are the words of a highly qualified geneticist and physician. This Bliss could have become your mitigating factor – if you'd returned to your senses the next day. But you chose to join them."

"Sorry for the slap – though, honestly, you had it coming. You drove me mad!" Sister Maria said, utterly unapologetic.

Selest coughed out her indignation. "*I* drove *you* mad? Unbelievable! I get it now. My Abeni is gone. She was witty, funny, a brilliant scientist, a dedicated colleague and a friend. I trusted her with my life."

Maria's expression softened, and she took a step closer. "I *am* your friend, Sel. My name may be different, my goals may be different, but that bond is still there. And I will save you."

Selest clenched her hands into fists. "Shut up," she hissed. "I would rather be buried in the ruins of civilisation than lose my mind like you."

They argued like this long into the night after the explosion outside.

At first, Selest pounded on the locked door, shouting, cursing and demanding her release. Then she fell into restless pacing, circling the room like a trapped animal. Finally, exhaustion forced her to collapse into a chair, unable to stop the tears – hot, angry and bitter. Not just for herself. For Aldo. For the life stolen from her a second time. For the friend she had lost long before this moment.

Maria watched in silence – calm, composed. She exhaled slowly, brushing non-existent dust from her sleeve as if waiting for her prisoner to catch up.

When Selest finally sat up, her face streaked with tears, Maria handed her a bottle of water. She hesitated but took it, drinking in one desperate gulp.

Maria smiled. "You see, sister? I'm still here for you."

"Don't." Selest's voice was hoarse. She wiped her mouth with the back of her hand, glaring. "You killed Aldo and his pilot. If you start preaching again, I swear I will—"

"I only want you to understand that I freed you from your capturers," Maria interrupted gently. "You wanted to escape, remember? Did they brainwash you into submission? I think you are lost, Sel. I can help you find your way."

Selest pressed her hands over her ears, gritting her teeth. "Fuck off, murderer!"

Maria only smiled – a genuine, almost sorrowful smile. "The famous words of the baby killer? I had hoped it wouldn't come to this," she murmured.

Selest barely had time to register the shift in tone before Maria turned to the door and knocked twice.

It opened instantly.

Two figures in flowing blue cloaks stepped inside. They moved with eerie synchronisation, their faces impassive.

Selest's muscles tensed, but strong hands seized her arms before she could react, pinning them in place. She thrashed, kicking out wildly, but they held firm.

Maria approached, a syringe glinting in her hand.

"Don't struggle," she said almost soothingly. "It's just a sedative. For now."

Selest jerked, trying to wrench free. "You crazy bitch—"

The needle slid into her vein with practised ease. Almost instantly, her limbs grew heavy, her vision blurring at the edges.

Maria's face swam in and out of focus, still wearing that same infuriatingly calm smile.

"Rest now," she murmured. "We have so much to talk about when you calm down."

Selest's world tilted and darkened.

She woke with the strange sensation of comfort – too much comfort. The sheets of real silk beneath her skin were impossibly soft, and the pleasant scent of ventilation filters lingered in the air. She could have believed she was back at the resort for a fleeting second, waking to another artificial sunrise, another day of carefully curated and comforting recreational activities. But as soon as she opened her eyes, reality crashed in.

There weren't even artificial windows in this room. The only light came from a large yellow oil lamp on the table.

She blinked, taking in her surroundings with growing unease. The room was spacious but mismatched.

A vanity with a tarnished mirror sat in the corner, its surface cluttered with trinkets – a silver comb, a broken clock, a porcelain figurine of a dancing woman missing an arm. A velvet theatre chair, darkened with age, faced a massive wooden wardrobe with intricately carved doors. The floor was covered by what had once been a luxurious carpet, its faded patterns eaten away by moths. And in the far corner stood a cluster of potted plants, their leaves withered, their branches brittle from years of neglect.

Selest breathed out sharply.

She knew who had once occupied this room. Or rather, what it had been before. The traces were unmistakable. This had once been Abeni's space. Now it belonged to Maria.

Selest's attention snapped to the heavy door. Of course it was locked. She was a prisoner. And if she was being held here – alone, untouched – it meant Maria still had plans for her.

She stepped into the adjoining bathroom and splashed water onto her face. The cold shock steadied her, but only slightly. She needed to think.

But the moment she re-entered the room, she froze.

A man was sitting in the velvet chair.

Tall, lean, exuding effortless poise. His long hair was neatly tied back, his face clean-shaven, his features striking – too symmetrical, too perfectly arranged, as though crafted for seduction. He might have been mistaken for a scholar or an actor were it not for how he held himself. His presence filled the room with something unspoken but deeply unsettling. A large cross around his neck looked completely out of place as if symbolising vulgarity.

On the table before him were two steaming mugs, the rich, unmistakable scent of coffee curling into the air. Real coffee. The kind that hadn't been brought to the resort in years.

The man gestured smoothly towards the cups.

"Good morning." His voice could make any woman's heart beat faster. "Maria said you take yours without sugar."

Selest didn't move.

Her mind flicked back to Abeni, to the way she had devoured every luxury back at the resort with defiance, protesting their captivity.

Selest stepped forwards, took one of the mugs, and lifted it to her lips. The aroma was intoxicating, and the taste was perfect.

And then, without breaking eye contact, she tilted her wrist and let the scorching liquid spill onto the carpet.

The man jerked his legs back just in time. The warmth in his expression vanished. Now everything he had planned to say would lose its power.

"I am disappointed," he said instead. "We had hoped you were civilised, a woman of reason, a representative of the elite class."

Selest arched an eyebrow. "Is that why you decided to try and bullshit me with pleasantries? Sebastian, right?"

His jaw tightened. Struggling for words was obviously a new sensation for him. This man wasn't used to being challenged like this.

"And if I refuse to listen to you?" she continued. "What then? Will you drug me? Break me? Tell me that ignorance is salvation, and that my place is beneath your god, beneath you?" She tilted her head. "Or are you just going to get it over with and rape me in a bathtub, telling me what to feel while you do it?"

The man's expression made her laugh – a sharp, bitter sound. She turned away from him, stepping towards the potted plants. She trailed her fingers along the brittle, dry leaves, feeling their lifelessness and fragility. Lemons or limes? They were dead – like every sense in this place.

Behind her, the man coughed, his voice cold now. "Then I have no choice but to tell you that I would gladly dispose of you myself. But

Maria," – he hesitated as if the name itself irritated him, – "for some reason, she believes you will see the light. That you will join us."

Selest didn't turn.

"You are too capable to be wasted," he continued. "Too skilful. You are an important piece of humanity's salvation. But first, the blasphemers must be purged. We will burn your nest of sinners."

The words made her stiffen, her jaw clenching tight.

"The Loaders must be destroyed," he finished as if reading out the verdict.

A chair scraped against the floor as he stood. Selest didn't move or breathe while the door opened, then closed with a quiet, decisive click.

Then she was alone.

She exhaled shakily. Think, Selest. Think.

She began to pace. The room was large, open enough for movement, but it was still a cage. No exits. No weapons. No tools. No way out.

Her friends, the children, Gleb – that sweet twelve-year-old boy she loved as if he were her son.

She pressed a fist against her lips, breathing through her nose to steady the tremor in her chest. She had failed them all.

She stopped.

Slowly, her focus returned to the lemon trees.

The lifeless branches, dry soil. The brown leaves curled like the husks of metamorphosed insects. Why were they still here? What drove Maria to keep what she once loved close to her, even if it was already dead?

A minute later, Selest knew what she had to do.

12: Farim

Sister Maria arrived a few hours later, carrying a tray with a steaming teapot, two cups and sandwiches filled with mushroom pâté and fresh greens. The pot smelled of mint – warm and soothing. Maria's voice was unnervingly casual, as if neither yesterday's events nor the last several years had ever happened.

"Sel, you must be hungry. Eat with me."

She glanced around the room. "It's been years since I stayed here. I have a better room now. Look at all this dust. By the way, this is all yours unless you want to be my room-mate."

Selest didn't feel hunger. She hadn't eaten in nearly a day, but grief and anxiety had twisted her stomach into a tight knot. The sight of food made her nauseous, but she obediently sat down, took a sandwich and bit into it.

Maria smiled, taking one for herself. "It's not caviar, but it's far more satiating. For dinner, we're having stew made of . . . well, perhaps it's better if you taste it first."

Selest silently finished her meal, then muttered, "Thank you, Maria."

"You're welcome. So, I take it you didn't like Sebastian?"

"Are you joking?" Selest scoffed. "Did you expect me to forget my circumstances and admire his Mr Smug Arse? Losing loved ones over and over again never becomes a habit, you know."

"I understand." Maria's voice was soft, almost pitying. "But if you look at loss from another perspective, it can bring – not relief, perhaps – but at least comfort. You grieve because your boyfriend is dead. But imagine . . . what if he's now somewhere far better?"

Selest's expression darkened. "Are you about to start preaching to me about the afterlife? Don't waste your breath."

Maria simply shrugged. "As you wish."

They finished the meal in silence. Then Maria picked up the tray and left.

She returned several hours later, though Selest couldn't say exactly how long it had been. This time, there was no tray in her hands. Instead, two men in blue robes followed her inside. Their hoods cast shadows over their serene, impassive expressions.

Maria's voice was almost cheerful. "Would you like to see our sanctuary?"

Selest picked up a small figurine from the vanity, then turned it over in her fingers. "Why would I? I know I'm in Montana now, and I'm just another doll in your collection."

"Well, I want to keep you from getting bored. And besides, I have a field hospital here. A patient needs your help – someone you can treat far better than I can."

Selest narrowed her eyes. "You're keeping me as a prisoner so I can work for you? Just like Dominic. You want me to heal your cultists?"

Maria remained unbothered. "He's severely burned, barely alive. He magically survived that thermocopter."

Selest's breath caught. She shot up from her seat. "Aldo?"

Sister Maria lifted a shoulder. "I don't know. I never met that man, even back at the resort. And besides . . . there's not much left of his face."

Selest was already moving towards the door, the two men falling in behind her. The hallway outside was stark and industrial, resembling maintenance corridors.

"Which way?" she demanded.

Maria led her past rows of doors, a gym and a hall converted into a chapel. The medical ward, however, was surprisingly modern. Two miserable young men sat beside a pregnant girl, speaking in hushed voices. Behind a privacy screen, a heavily bandaged figure lay motionless.

"I did what I could," Maria said, watching Selest closely. "But he'll need skin grafts. If you agree to do this, we'll get what you need. Trust me – I'm a doctor."

"Abeni was a doctor," Selest said bitterly. "Shouldn't Sister Maria renounce her former profession and pray for God's mercy?"

Maria's jaw tightened. "This *is* an act of mercy. I remember the pain of burns all too well. And though this blasphemer may have deserved it, we always offer even the most lost a chance to return to God."

The man was the same height and build as Aldo, but that wasn't unusual – most resort guards were tall and athletic. His injuries were severe, leaving little for Selest to identify. She knew Aldo's hands intimately – every birthmark, every line of his skin. But this man had no hair left, and his skin was blistered. Without modern treatments – dermo-rep gel and advanced stem cell dressings designed to accelerate healing – he wouldn't have survived.

Selest spent the next several weeks caring for the patient. At first, he was more dead than alive, his body terribly weakened. She cleaned his wounds, replaced bandages and adjusted the IVs that kept him hydrated and nourished. She could not access some of the advanced equipment she once used. She relied mostly on what Cruisers managed to supply and her manual care, patience and time. Growing skin culture here was possible but not perfect. She had no means for any feature reconstruction. She managed to save one of his eyes, although it had lost its pigment and needed regular maintenance.

When the man regained consciousness, this colourless eye flickered open, clouded with pain and disorientation. Selest leaned over him, heart pounding.

"Aldo?" she asked softly.

His features sharpened slightly, focusing on her face. He looked as if he were struggling to gather his thoughts. A groan of realisation and sorrow escaped his lips as he lifted his disfigured, bandaged hands to his eyes. Then he sighed, his voice more like the rustle of paper. "I am not . . ."

The words felt like a blade to her chest.

He swallowed and added, "I guess Aldo didn't make it."

Selest stared at him, her mind struggling to grasp the reality she had refused to consider. She had held on to hope, believing – no, needing – to believe that Aldo had survived. And now she was mourning him all over again.

She pressed her palms together, willing herself to stay steady. "Then, you are his . . ."

He exhaled a shaky breath. "Farim. I was the pilot. You remember me, Ms Dvali?"

She remembered. Farim – tall, strong but quiet, competent, always focused on his job. She hadn't known him well, but she recalled his face. Or rather, what his face used to be.

Now he was a ruin of the man he once was, his features distorted by burns, his body barely holding together. His remaining eye, the other completely destroyed in the crash. Yet, in this place he was her only connection to the life she had lost. Soon she would have to tell him what had happened and where they were.

Swallowing her grief, she nodded. "Farim, do you feel any pain? If yes, where?"

"Everywhere. My right shoulder hurts the most . . . and my jaw."

"Thank you. Don't worry, I have painkillers. I'll take care of you. Now rest, Farim. We'll talk later."

Over the following days, she continued to treat him, monitoring his recovery. His skin was a patchwork of healing grafts, and his hands were functional but difficult to use properly. When she and Maria finally managed to reconstruct his face enough for it to be humanlike, he asked for something to conceal it.

"I need something to cover my head," he murmured, his voice thick with exhaustion.

Selest hesitated, then turned to Maria.

Maria considered him for a moment before nodding. "Fine. I'll give you one of our robes."

A few hours later, she returned with a long blue hooded coat and a full face mask – the same ones worn by the followers of her sect. She set them down beside the bed.

"There," she said simply. "You will look like a Cruiser a bit too early, but you can hide your scars."

Farim reached for the mask with trembling fingers. Selest watched him carefully – she couldn't tell if he was relieved, grateful or resigned.

But she did know one thing.

He was the only person in this place who wasn't lost to Sister Maria's faith. For now, that was enough. For how long, though, before they preached to him too?

He took the news of their imprisonment in silence, thought about it, and then said, "They can try. This will be interesting."

Farim eventually recovered, but once he regained strength, he became a stealthy yet steady presence in Selest's life. They formed a bond – one of whispered secrets and shared glances, a dangerous friendship hidden beneath the weight of watchful eyes.

The sect wasted no time trying to claim him. Father Sebastian had spoken with him, leaning in with the gravity of a man who had delivered this speech a thousand times before. He told Farim that his suffering was no accident – that it was the result of blasphemy, sin and the corruption of his past life. The fire that nearly consumed him was a cleansing, and his survival was a gift from the Lord – a second chance, a path to salvation.

Selest warned her new friend as she sat close to his bed under the dim light of the infirmary. "Agree with them. Pretend you are listening more and thinking less, but don't let it in," she murmured. "Remember, it's all manipulation. The explosion was their doing.

They don't care about redemption. They need obedient soldiers and expendable bodies."

Farim nodded. He played his part well. He bowed his head when expected, repeated the prayers and let them believe he was coming into the fold.

Selest did the same in her own way. Sister Maria visited her often, speaking with a warmth that would have been touching if it hadn't been for the chains binding Selest to this place.

"I never abandoned you," Maria would say, eyes soft with emotion. "You are my friend, and I love you so much! I want to see you safe. I want us to be sisters."

At first, Selest would act irritated and resistant herself. She would scowl, fold her arms – but she wouldn't pull away when Maria took her hand and pressed it to her chest. She even let Maria embrace her once.

A slow, tentative gesture.

That was how survival worked. Deep down, Selest couldn't help but marvel at the contradiction. Despite their cunning and audacity in seizing power and battling the resistance of intelligent, rational minds, their belief that they could simply talk people into submission was almost naive. Yet perhaps that was the key to their rapid growth. No amount of reason could stand unshaken against relentless demagoguery and arguments built entirely on fallacy. Preying on vulnerability also worked magic in this place.

In time, Selest pieced together where they were. The corridors, the crumbling lecture halls with their hollowed-out bookshelves – it was a Havre college, long abandoned and repurposed into something far more insidious. The sect had claimed it as their own, filling the empty halls with murmured prayers and quiet fanaticism.

Eventually, Farim was assigned to work servicing the sect's few transport vehicles. It gave him a role in the settlement, and more importantly, it kept him away from the worst of their sermons. Selest saw him only during medical check-ups, when he would sit before her, letting her examine his healing skin and reconstructed hands.

She sighed one afternoon as she removed the last of his bandages. "Soon I'll have to declare you healthy. You won't have any reason to come here any more. And our rooms are still guarded."

"That's all right, Doctor. We'll meet in the laundry hall during washing shifts. The machines are loud, and no one lingers there. Apparently, washing blue robes is far less important to these people than cleansing their souls."

She smirked despite herself. Farim's voice had a quality to it now, like a bird's quiet warble.

And so, time passed. Weeks turned into months. And then came the night of the Cruisers' Induction Ceremony.

Selest arrived at their secret meeting place first, slipping into the shadows of an empty supply room. Farim came a few moments later.

She handed him a syringe. "This is an antidote to Bliss. Inject it an hour before the ceremony. Make sure no one sees."

Farim turned the vial between his fingers. The sect's favoured drug – Bliss – wasn't just a sedative. It induced euphoria, heightened suggestibility, and, most of all, complete submission. It would be given to everyone – initiates and seasoned believers alike – tonight.

Including Sister Maria. Including Father Sebastian.

"Do you know what to do if we have a chance to get away?" Farim asked. "I have made some preparations just in case."

"Yes, but will we have that chance?"

"We can at least try." He smiled, though he could do it with only half his face. "We are not too far from the North Montana Trading Post; we should go there and hide. One day, someone from the Resistance will come."

And so, when the ceremony began, they were the only ones who remained clear-headed.

The induction took place in what had once been an indoor swimming pool, now transformed into a murky pond. The water was far from clean, its surface broken by wild aquatic plants thriving under the occasional light through a transparent polymer ceiling. The night storm was drumming into it. Towering walls, once bare, were now adorned with ancient banners, their fabric embroidered with sacred verses. Along the edges, candles flickered, their wax dripping onto the cold stone, casting trembling shadows over the gathered faithful.

The initiates – men and women alike – were led forwards first, dressed in the same blue robes as the rest of the sect. They kneeled in neat rows by the pool, hands pressed to their chests, heads bowed. One by one, an injection was administered into the vessels at their necks.

Then the others joined, their movements slow and dreamlike. The air thickened with murmured prayers and whispered hymns. It felt more like a fever dream than a ritual.

Selest and Farim stood among them, their expressions carefully neutral. They played their parts. And watched as the humble, silent crowd became something else entirely.

At first, it was a mass of swaying bodies, hands raised in devotion. Then the ceremony unravelled into something looser, more chaotic. The sect moved like a tide – touching, embracing, lips meeting lips, hands roaming over fabric and bare skin.

It was no longer a ceremony. It was an orgy.

Some equipment must have been hidden somewhere behind the banners because, as soon as Sebastian finished his impassioned speech, music filled the hall – something from the past, heavy and primal, wild and unsettling. His words echoed: people are God's children, and parents forgive their children. The natural, organic, original and pure is the only path to our Father, our only Lord.

The gathering erupted. Clothes were torn away, limbs entangled and men and women chased each other like frenzied beasts. They howled, squealed and dropped to the floor in a writhing, mindless dance. Some leaped into the water, splashing like children in the murky pond, laughing and shrieking under the candlelight.

A man grabbed Selest by the sleeves and pulled, his breath hot and eager, but Farim moved before she had time to react. He threw back his hood, revealing the wreckage of his burned face. The man recoiled in dismay and vanished into the thrashing crowd.

Selest turned and checked the pond where Sebastian and Maria, already naked, were locked in an eerie, slow kiss, standing waist-deep in water. Maria's face was flushed, her pupils wide as she clung to Father Sebastian, whispering something against his neck. He smiled, brushing her hair back, his eyes unfocused. Once they were done with each other, they would take on Selest and give her a new name. She knew it.

Selest turned away, heart pounding.

Farim whistled with surprise beside her. "I think I preferred when they were just praying," he murmured.

Selest looked around and said, "We can't stay here much longer." She let her blue robe slip from her shoulders and turned to Farim. "Carry me away from here. They need to believe we're doing what they are doing."

For now, they had won this small battle – they had resisted Bliss and kept their minds clear – but neither was safe as long as they stayed in this place.

Farim understood. He was strong enough by now. Without hesitation, he hoisted Selest over his shoulder and pushed through the tangled mass of bodies, shoving aside those who stood in his way. The hallway was just as chaotic – three young bodies lay entwined in passion right at the door. He nearly stumbled over them but regained his footing, turning sharply towards the stairwell.

Only when they reached the landing did he set her down.

"This is our chance. The garage!" she urged.

But he didn't move.

His grip on her hand tightened, fingers lingering as if unwilling to let go. He stepped closer. She felt his hot, heavy breath against her neck – but it wasn't from running.

A chill slithered down her spine. The antidote . . . was it wearing off?

"Come on," she whispered, covering herself and pulling him towards the exit.

For a moment, he stayed still. Then, with a sharp inhale, he blinked himself back to reality, donned his mask and followed Selest into the night.

The storm had only worsened since dusk. The wind howled through the abandoned grounds, tearing at their robes and drowning out the noise inside the building.

They reached the lot where nine trucks and cars sat in the dark. Farim helped her remove the bolts from the gate without a word, then grabbed a crowbar from a nearby tool shed. He moved methodically, wasting no time – puncturing the tyres of electric cars, ripping out wires, smashing batteries and converters. Selest didn't have a mask, so she wasn't much help, trying to cover her face with a scrap of blue fabric.

He slashed open the fuel tanks of two ancient trucks, the sharp scent of petrol cutting through the cold air.

Only then did he climb into the last intact vehicle. With a rough turn of the ignition, the truck roared to life.

Selest jumped into the passenger seat just as he slammed the doors shut. With a final glance at the hell they were leaving behind, Farim stepped on the accelerator.

The truck lurched forwards, its tyres kicking up sand and gravel.

They sped through the night, heading west – leaving Havre and crossing the continent along the broad and straight US-2.

13: Root Town

As they travelled westwards, the landscape transformed. The vast, open plains gradually gave way to the rising contours of the mountains, their low, jagged silhouettes rippling against the horizon. The wind, which had howled fiercely the night before, had softened to a restless murmur, stirring the dust along the road. By the time they passed Browning, the first light of dawn revealed an extraordinary sight ahead.

The colossal Eight Trees of Kiowa City.

Selest had been up the Two Tree

shopping centre near her home town and read about other giant trees, but nothing had prepared her for the sheer scale of the arboreal specimens before her. The smallest of the eight had a trunk nearly a half kilometre in diameter, its canopy so vast it could swallow an entire city block in shadow. Towering higher than any skyscraper humans had ever constructed, their immense limbs intertwined like living bridges in the sky. These were not natural wonders in the old sense – mutation, climate shifts and human interference had created them hundreds of years ago. No man-made buildings could lift human habitation above the global smog and dust storms.

The highest reaches of the trees, above the dirt and dust, were reserved for the privileged residents of Crown Town, connected by intricate lifts and railway bridges built into the bark. But down at the base, among the gnarled roots, sprawled Root Town – a settlement built in the undergrowth, where those without wealth or status eked out their existence.

Selest and Farim had no choice but to arrive at ground level.

Here, makeshift shacks leaned against the colossal roots, their wooden frames reinforced with salvaged metal and tattered tarps. The pathways between them were narrow and winding, lit by strings of dim electric lights powered by wind turbines above. The people moved slowly, without hurry or purpose, their lives dictated by the twilight world beneath the canopy.

Farim had made an error in his escape preparations. He had thought of bringing Selest alternative clothes, and now she was dressed in a worn-out jumpsuit from her old life. But he still wore his blue Cruiser robe, its hood and mask concealing his identity. Farim was reluctant, though, to take it off.

"I'm more likely to startle them with my face than my colours, Ms Dvali," he had reasoned.

Selest had disagreed. And she had been right.

As they cautiously approached the edge of the settlement, the quiet buzz of daily life slowed. Conversations dulled to whispers. The scrape of wood against wood ceased as workers paused, tools still in their hands. A group of children, previously playing near the roots, stopped and stared. A stove crackled somewhere inside one of the shacks, and the scent of burning bark drifted through the dry air.

Selest stepped forwards, keeping her posture relaxed.

"Greetings," she said evenly. "We are travellers seeking refuge and information. Might we speak with someone in charge?"

A few glances were exchanged. A long

wooden pole shifted in one man's grip. Another fingered the edge of a woodsman's axe. Out of the corner of her eye, Selest noticed that Farim made a strange gesture as if he had grabbed something from his chest and tossed it away. Then, a moment later, a tall man nodded.

"Come with me," he said.

They followed him through the winding paths until they reached a larger structure built directly into the base of one of the giant trees. Inside, the air was cool and dim, beams of yellow light filtering through uneven planks.

The older man, dressed in worn-out clothing, motioned for them to stop as they entered and introduced themselves. "What do you want? If you've come to preach, you can leave right now."

Farim peacefully raised both hands. "We are not Cruisers," he said. "We were their prisoners. They tried to break us, to make us submit. But we refused. Now we are refugees, seeking knowledge of the Resistance."

The man studied them, his expression far from friendly. A long silence stretched between them. Then he finally said, "I am Eldrin, the landlord of these quarters. And if you're lying? That robe is a little too convenient for your story."

Selest narrowed her eyes. "You're quick to distrust, but look at what they did to him. Farim, show him."

Farim hesitated. Then, slowly, he reached up and removed his mask.

Selest had expected disgust, perhaps even pity. She did not anticipate how Eldrin's eyes widened in sheer fascination.

"Wow!" The man called Eldrin took an unconscious step forwards. "I – I am lost for words. Farim, is that your name, boy? My word, you are beautiful."

Selest and Farim both blinked in surprise.

"Are you like this all the way, or just . . . ?" Eldrin gestured vaguely, clearly trying to suppress his excitement. Then, suddenly remembering himself, he cleared his throat and stepped back. "Ah – where are my manners? Please, sit."

Eldrin was a wiry, weathered man, his leathery skin carved with age. Sparse grey hair framed sharp hazel eyes that were always darting with cunning. He provided them with food – simple but hearty: flatbread, roasted beetroots and a thick stew rich with the earthy flavour of mushrooms. Selest ate slowly, her senses still on edge, listening intently as the landlord spoke.

"We don't see many outsiders here," Eldrin admitted, tearing a piece of bread and dipping it into his bowl. "And certainly not ones who look like this young man." He gestured at Farim with a crooked grin.

Selest's curiosity sharpened. "Why does

his appearance matter so much?"

Eldrin's expression was one of delight rather than marvel. "Because I am an artist and have a good eye for uniqueness. And I've never seen anything quite like him before. My models all look almost the same – strong jaws, faces marked by trouble and memories, the same old stories written in their wrinkles. But you, my boy . . ." He leaned forwards slightly, assessing Farim with a gleam of inspiration in his eye. "You're different. You have a face that demands to be captured. I shall paint you in watercolour and ink. Yes! Tell me, Farim. Do you sit for portraits?"

Farim frowned, his single brow knitting over his only eye. "You want to paint me?"

"Only if you allow it," Eldrin assured him. "As a token of goodwill, I'll find you a proper house, a job and a place in our little community."

Selest decided to make it clear. "We need

information," she said bluntly. "This place serves as an exchange post for the Resistance. We want to know when you expect them next. Considering your reaction to Farim's blue robe, I assume you don't support the Cruisers?"

"That's right, we don't," Eldrin confirmed, his tone firm. "But it's never that simple. The Resistance don't plan their visits openly or stick to predictable schedules. It would be too easy for someone to betray them. They come in different vehicles, at varying times, with no patterns whatsoever. Sometimes months pass without a visit; other times, they show up less than a week after their last exchange. They trade supplies, but for sensitive information. They use the Multiplanetary Encrypted Synchronisation Hub."

"The MESH?" Selest asked, the sharp memory of the dish-like antenna at the Ozhogino resort flashing through her mind.

"That's right. The Cruisers have no

access to it – they call it an ungodly device, a sinful corruption. But the Resistance relies on it. They didn't stay more than four hours the last time they were here. That was only a couple of weeks ago." Eldrin gestured towards the remaining bread on the table. "They bring us food in exchange for the spores we grow deep underground. But mostly, their resources go to the privileged ones," he added, glancing meaningfully at the ceiling.

"Spores?" Farim asked, looking to Selest for clarification. "Some sort of fungus?"

"*Resuscitatus miraculum*," Selest explained. "Still one of the most effective strains for antibiotic production, mainly because it mutates almost as fast as harmful bacteria."

This time Eldrin looked genuinely impressed. "Are you a pharmacist or a doctor?"

"Used to be a neurosurgeon," Selest said, frowning slightly as she thought about it. It felt like another life entirely.

"Then you're more than welcome to stay with us," Eldrin declared. "We've got sick people here who could use your help."

Selest studied him carefully. "I'll see what I can do," she said at last. "But only if you give us access to your MESH. I assume you must have one here if you trade with the Resistance?"

Eldrin chuckled. "Smart girl. But all the equipment is up there." He tilted his head upwards again. "I use it only when we need something."

"Do you have a permit to get up to the Crown?" Farim asked.

"No, but I know a secret way."

Selest exchanged glances with Farim. Crown Town was said to be nearly impossible to reach without the right status or connections. If Eldrin truly had a hidden way in, that could change everything.

"A secret way?" Selest pressed.

Eldrin smirked. "Oh yes, Doc. The trees are old. Their insides aren't as solid as they used to be. Some of us know paths that others don't. So – what do you say? I'll pass on a message to the Resistance for you. If they come, they come. In the meantime, you stay here, wait, and" – he tapped the side of his nose – "you, young lady, will look after our sick. And you" – he turned to Farim – "will model for me . . . in the nude! Well . . . almost."

Farim sat back, considering.

"Fine," he said, his voice flat. "You'll get your painting, but only if you don't make it ridiculous."

Eldrin grinned. "Oh, I assure you, I take my work very seriously."

Selest watched Eldrin closely, measuring his words. The old landlord was canny – he understood the value of what he was offering and was leveraging it well.

She took another mouthful of the thick

stew, letting the taste settle on her tongue. They needed a foothold here, and as much as she disliked the idea of waiting, she saw no other option. If the Resistance were as unpredictable as Eldrin claimed, they had no choice but to bide their time.

"I need to make sure you pass on the message," Selest said finally. "If they do not come, we will leave anyway."

"As you wish, Doc?" Eldrin wiped his hands on a towel. "I will not keep you against your will. I am not a Cruiser. But if you are considering going up there, you better think twice. It is not a pleasure trip."

Selest didn't answer and Eldrin continued. "People at the top don't collaborate with Cruisers, but they are snobs. How do you think they get rid of their waste?" He glanced towards the ceiling again. "It all ends up here, and we fertilise our farms. There are old sewage tunnels in the cores, some natural, some artificial and most abandoned or forgotten. Some are dangerous – collapsing or filled with who knows what? But some are just inconvenient, and all we had to do is ensure the ladders still hold."

"And you know the one that is merely convenient," Farim said drily.

Eldrin grinned. "Naturally."

Selest sighed. This was promising. If they could reach Crown Town unnoticed, they might also use the MESH to contact Dominic and warn him.

"I will take my chances and come with you," she said. "And I'll see your unwell tenants afterwards."

Eldrin nodded, satisfied. "We will start very early tomorrow, Doc. Get some rest tonight. There's a spare shack two rows down. It's not luxurious, but it's sturdy and dry."

Selest didn't protest. They had spent too long in the truck, and exhaustion was beginning to settle into her bones. The promise of a solid surface to sleep on, even if it was just wooden planks, was enough.

The shack was smaller than she expected, little more than a rectangle of scrap wood and tarpaulin wedged between two enormous roots. Inside was a single cot, a wooden bench and a crate that served as a table. A faint scent of earth filled the air, though at least the roof seemed intact.

Farim leaned against the wall, pulling off his robe at last. The dim light made his scars seem deeper, his single eye shadowed.

"Do you trust him, Ms Dvali?" he asked.

Selest sat on the cot and began unlacing her boots. "Not entirely. But he has no reason to sell us out. If he works with the Resistance, he's better off keeping us as allies. And since we moved in together, you can call me Selest."

Farim let out a quiet sigh. "And the painting?"

Selest smirked. "That's your problem."

He rolled his eye. "You're heartless."

She lay back on the cot, stretching out. The wood was hard beneath her, but it was a bed. "He's giving us a way in. If that means you have to sit quiet and half naked for a few hours, then so be it."

Farim made a noncommittal sound as he stretched on the wooden floor.

Outside, the wind rustled through the leaves above them, creating a distant, whispering hush. The shacks of Root Town were mostly silent now, the occasional murmur of conversation filtering through the thin walls.

"If I get to a terminal, I'll try to contact the resort and warn them," Selest said quietly.

"You won't succeed. Eternum Project does not exist for ordinary folks," Farim said in a tired voice from the floor.

"And how do you contact Dominic when you visit the trading posts?"

"Search for his nickname account. There will be a password for the messages. I'll tell you it tomorrow."

"Dominic has a nickname among his guards?" Selest said with surprise.

"Yes. It was the same for years. But the password changes from time to time. Look for Dome-and-Dick . . . hey! Don't laugh!"

Selest giggled again and then turned onto her side, closing her eyes. The journey westwards had been relentless; she had expected signs of pursuit at any moment through it. Now she felt safe enough to sleep for the first time since their escape.

Tomorrow would be an important day.

14: Crown Town

The next day started early, and it was still dark when Eldrin led them to a dimly lit chamber. An old oil lamp flickered against the wooden walls, casting long shadows. The room smelled of ink and aged paper, and stacks of canvases leaned in the corners. At the centre stood a chair draped with a faded embroidered cloth.

"This is where I work," Eldrin announced theatrically. "I want to make a first sketch as soon as you, my dear boy, take your shirt off."

Farim tensed visibly. "Really?"

"You've been hiding under that robe for too long. It's time to cast off the curse. You are not a monster. You are a masterpiece!" Eldrin declared, his tone both reassuring and firm. "And don't worry – I said *almost* nude. Just pull up your trousers. Drapery adds mystery."

Farim rolled his eye and pulled off his robe, exposing the patchwork of scars and grafted skin. Selest felt a pang of guilt at the sight of her own rushed work, but Eldrin only sucked in a breath.

"My word . . . your body is a landscape of its own," he murmured, fingers twitching for his brush. "I could make a hundred paintings of you, and each would tell a different story."

Farim sat heavily on the chair. "Just don't

make me look . . . pitiful."

Eldrin's eyes gleamed. "Pitiful? With those muscles? No. This will be a portrait of defiance." He gestured towards the doorway. "Ah, and here are the new clothes you'll wear afterwards."

A young woman entered, carrying a neat pile of garments. She was tall and graceful, her golden curls cascading down her back. Dressed in trousers and a long shirt, a rucksack slung over her shoulder, she had an air of firm confidence. Her sharp, inquisitive eyes locked onto Farim, widening with fascination. She had a charming face, though not perfectly symmetrical – one eye sat slightly lower than the other, and her mouth tugged left whenever she smiled.

"This is my beautiful grand-granddaughter, Kaelin," Eldrin said with a wink. "She'll be escorting the brave doctor to the Crown and the terminals. I'm too old to climb that far, and I'm keen to start my art project. You ladies, leave now. He needs to relax, and we have work to do."

Kaelin's cheeks flushed slightly, but she held her ground. Selest recognised in her expression the same admiration Eldrin had shown. The girl lingered for a moment longer, then turned to Selest.

"Pleased to meet you, Doctor. Come – we have a long climb ahead."

Selest glanced at Farim. He looked uneasy but gave her a small nod of encouragement. With that, she followed Kaelin out of the room, leaving Eldrin and Farim alone. Amid the swirl of emotions, one flitted past like a fly: the thought that she would never see Farim again. She waved it aside and hurried after the girl.

The sunrise was still hours away, and the alleys of Root Town twisted and turned like an endless maze. Kaelin's lantern barely illuminated their path. The undercanopy was dense, the air thick with damp wood and the faint scent of smoke from unseen fires.

The way up was nothing like Selest had imagined. It was a hidden route, carved into the very fabric of the tree, with ladder brackets embedded in one side. She had seen similar ladders outside factory chimneys.

"You don't use sewage pipes?" Selest asked as they entered the hollowed-out trunk.

Kaelin laughed softly, tying her long hair into a tight bun at the back of her head. "That's just a joke my grand-grandfather likes to tell. No, we climb the builders' shafts. They're hardly used these days."

And climb they did. It wasn't a simple ascent up ladders or makeshift scaffolding. The pathway led them through ancient tunnels, spiralling upwards inside the massive tree. As they climbed higher, the passageways became sturdier, reinforced by careful engineering – a seamless fusion of nature and human ingenuity. Though both young women were strong, the climb was long and exhausting, with many stops to rest their limbs before they finally reached the Crown.

Kaelin's key unlocked a hatch, and a moment later, they stepped onto the floor of what looked like a house basement – an abandoned old laundry room.

"If we want to blend in, we need the right clothes," Kaelin said, pulling two elegant dresses from a rucksack. The fabric shimmered under the dim light, finely made and tailored for a life far removed from the harsh realities below.

Selest ran her fingers over the smooth folds of white and gold. "I missed this," she admitted.

"Then wear it."

With Kaelin's help, she changed into the dress, adjusting a large hat and visor that concealed most of her face.

Kaelin dressed too, slipping into a pale-silver gown before nodding approvingly.

Selest frowned, shifting uncomfortably. "This is the strangest outfit I've ever worn. I've had visors in my travel gear but never attached to fancy hats and festive dresses. Is the air here dusty too?"

"They don't need them," Kaelin said, her voice dripping with contempt. "It's just fashion – a way to show 'solidarity' with the suffering world. But in reality, it's a joke. You've been away too long, Doctor. Now follow me. Keep your head down, walk calmly and don't speak to anyone. Here, people mostly know each other."

As they emerged onto the upper levels, Selest finally saw Crown Town. It was breathtaking – unlike the commercial centre on her home town's solitary giant tree.

A city of gleaming polymer walls and domes stretched above the canopy, its structures linked by suspended bridges and walkways. Multistorey buildings had been seamlessly integrated with the colossal tree, a perfect blend of technology and nature. It looked almost utopian – until one considered how exclusive it all was.

"You look surprised," Kaelin noted.

"It's been a long time since I've been on a

tree like this," Selest admitted. "My one was called Two Tree Market because it was split in the middle, with buildings between the two trunks. Dominic Veir designed it. He designed these cities, too, didn't he?"

Kaelin tilted her head. "Yes. There are two cities like this, plus six single trees across different parts of Earth. You know of Veir?"

Selest hesitated. "I used to work for him."

A flicker of strong emotion crossed Kaelin's face, but she said nothing. Instead, she led Selest between two larger structures, their dresses flowing behind them as they stepped deeper into the heart of Crown Town.

The city in the trees was eerily quiet. Few people roamed the streets, and those who did seemed entirely absorbed in their own affairs. Men and women wore elegant clothing as if attending a masquerade ball, their faces partially obscured. Above them, the transparent polymer dome filtered the sunlight, casting everything in a soft, ethereal glow. The air was rich with oxygen and free of impurities – pristine, artificial perfection.

"Trees on the trees," Selest murmured, nodding towards several olive trees in large pots.

"This is nothing," Kaelin responded. "You should see the lilac alley on the eucalyptus at the southern edge – or the orchids on the eastern chestnut."

"What tree is this?"

"The larch."

Eventually, they arrived at a grand hall with rows of terminals, each mounted on short columns. People sat before them, their eyes fixed on holographic screens displaying an endless stream of entertainment, data and communications.

"This is the Universal Stock Pavilion," Kaelin explained, activating a terminal for her own task. "It includes MESH access to music, films, novel archives and personal accounts. If you need to contact someone, do it here."

Selest approached an unoccupied terminal, hesitating before entering her secure personal credentials. A glint of disbelief passed through her as the screen loaded. Everything was still there – her correspondence, work records, saved videoflickers and articles . . . remnants of her old life.

Selest let out a quiet laugh when she searched for Dominic Veir's private handle and entered the password. The request processed.

"Will it work?" she asked Kaelin.

"We'll have to wait. But once you start, don't take too long – someone will detect it. I already sent a message to the Resistance, saying we have a lost doctor. If you told us the truth, they'll know exactly what I mean."

Minutes passed. Selest grew restless. Just as she was about to give up, the screen blinked to life. Dominic Veir appeared, looking tired but unharmed. She lifted her visors to greet him.

"Selest?" His eyes widened. "You're alive."

"Dominic," she breathed. "I need to tell you what happened, but I don't know how much time I have."

She quickly summarised their kidnapping, Aldo's death, Farim's misfortune, the cult, their recruitment tactics and the looming threat against the resort. Dominic listened in silence, his expression growing darker with each detail.

"The resort is still secure," he assured her. "But I won't take any chances. I'll start evacuating the young Loaders immediately."

Before she could respond, a flashing red alert appeared on the screen.

Kaelin tensed beside her. "We need to go," she whispered.

Selest turned back to the display. "Dominic, is everything all right with Gleb and—"

The connection cut abruptly.

She stiffened, scanning her surroundings. A pair of uniformed men had entered the hall and were now making their way towards them, their strides deliberate.

"Log off and come on," Kaelin said with a hiss, grabbing Selest's wrist and pulling her visors down again. "Walk slowly, like a curious bystander."

They moved towards the nearest exit, arm in arm. Selest forced herself to appear calm, but Kaelin faltered first. Panic whitened the girl's lips, and she suddenly pulled her hand away, sprinting into the nearest alley.

The guards reacted instantly. They broke into a run, chasing after her.

Selest froze, unsure of what to do. Around her, a small group of pavilion visitors murmured, watching the commotion. She had lost her bearings – this place was an intricate maze of platforms, multi-levelled streets and suspended walkways. She had no idea which way they had entered from.

Moments later, the guards emerged from the alley alone. Kaelin had vanished.

The onlookers began to disperse, leaving Selest standing awkwardly in the open. She needed to avoid suspicion. Without another option, she returned to the terminal, logged into the MESH and accessed the public news feed.

At first, she merely skimmed, trying to calm herself. But soon the headlines pulled her into what she already knew but rarely had the chance to watch, being trapped in Ozhogino.

In the years she had spent underground, the world had changed at an astonishing pace – faster and more drastically than she had imagined. Religious movements had surged in power, sweeping entire nations, seizing governments and rewriting laws. Young anarchists, disillusioned with the constraints of civilisation, had flocked to these radical sects, drawn by the promise of chaos and reckless freedom. "Live today, for there is no tomorrow!" they chanted, blind to the destruction they enabled.

In densely populated areas of Europe, lawlessness had taken hold. Gangs roamed the highways in stolen vehicles, plundering settlements too weak to defend themselves. Property rights and societal structures were crumbling, leaving fewer and fewer people willing – or even able – to uphold the values of knowledge, skill and progress.

Selest slowly shook her head, fingers tightening around the edge of the terminal. Society itself was rotting from within, swollen with decay, corroding like an iron tool left to rust. And yet, somewhere beneath the corrosion, a core of resilience remained.

The Resistance had grown. An army of space marines had joined their ranks. Even if Earth was slipping through their grasp, those across the solar system still fought to preserve civilisation's last threads.

Under her breath, she whispered, "Fear is an ancient weapon . . . monstrously effective. We once thought the Platinum Age would never end, that the world would never return to barbarism. How wrong we were. But where did we make our greatest mistake?"

"In education," a female voice answered behind her. "Fear is a natural instinct that ensures self-preservation, but the ability to control it must be cultivated."

Selest turned sharply and found herself face to face with a tall woman clad in a bronze velvet uniform, its fabric shimmering under the dim lamplight. In stark contrast, the buttons were matte black – like bullet holes scattered across her chest. Her face was handsome, but her eyes were lifeless. Artificial irises. The unique, glassy sheen of her corneas gave her away. She was blind – likely from birth – her vision granted only through technology.

The woman raised her fist to her chest as if clutching an invisible medallion or a crucifix. Selest recognised the gesture. She had seen Farim do the same. Instinctively, she mirrored the movement. Then, in unison, they both mimed tearing the invisible object away and discarding it.

Understanding dawned. This woman was a high-ranking member of the Resistance, someone who had no interest in humanity slipping back into the dark ages. After all, the gift of sight was too precious to be sacrificed to the delusions of divine providence.

"You have the eyes of a Loader," Selest observed. "And I even know who designed them – eighteen years ago."

"My father," the woman replied.

"Thanks to his work, I can see right through you. Literally. And you seem to know it."

"You're able to scan and compare facial structures—" Selest began but stopped herself.

"And confirm that you are Doctor Dvali, officially presumed dead. Twice," the woman finished for her.

Selest nodded, her mind racing. "And you are Xenia Westwind, daughter of Professor Veodoro Westwind. I only attended his private lectures four times – and then only as a reward."

"So we can skip formal introductions," Xenia said with a polite but distant smile. "You warned Ozhogino about the sect's attack. You may have saved many lives. Follow me. We'll be more comfortable speaking in my office."

Selest hesitated. "How did you find out so quickly?"

"Mr Veir contacted me just minutes ago. I was equally surprised to learn that the message came from my city."

Selest narrowed her eyes. "So, the city of snobs in the trees is actually a Resistance stronghold? We thought it was just an exchange post, a sanctuary for aristocrats who prefer to remain ignorant of the world's decline."

Xenia stopped at the pavilion exit and turned to face her. "That's a good thing," she said. "Eighty per cent of Kiowa's residents are, in fact, blissfully unaware of reality. But what difference does that make? That's precisely how the society of the whole planet has functioned for the last five hundred years."

She resumed slow walking, but Selest felt she had to hurry to keep up.

"But what about the people in Root Town?" Selest pressed. "They're rebels against mysticism too. Why don't you bring them up here? Their lives would improve."

Xenia didn't even glance back. "That's impossible. Their work is vital to Kiowa's economy. We no longer rely on Montana's government for aid, and self-sufficiency is a great temptation for the Thieves. The fewer people who know about our true operations, the lower the risk of betrayal or espionage. Keeping them where they are is a necessary security measure."

Selest frowned. "But Kiowa isn't overcrowded. There's space here. I thought every dedicated rebel would be worth their weight in gold these days."

Xenia's voice turned cold. "We provide them with food and medicine. They believe it comes from the Resistance. Doctor, you're hardly in a position to lecture me on morality. If we speak in the language of mystics, your sins are greater than mine."

Selest stiffened.

Xenia continued, her tone cutting. "We all do what is necessary for humanity to survive. You create Loaders. I ensure the safety of those who can change something in this catastrophe. The mystics believe these trees are an abomination. Someday, they will burn them down – along with the people and the architecture. But right now, that's not their priority. And I intend to keep it that way for as long as possible."

Selest halted abruptly. "How will you protect the Eternum Project?"

Xenia stopped as well, then turned slightly. "I've already reported to the landing base and sent an agent to infiltrate the Cruisers. He will determine when they make their move.

Squads will arrive in Ozhogino in two days to assist with the evacuation."

Selest pressed a cold hand to her burning cheek. "But too much time has passed since the initiation. If they hadn't wasted time searching for Farim and me, they could already be approaching Western Alaska with their ground transports. I have to go there. Now."

Xenia studied her for a moment, then nodded. "Someone is already there to greet them. But if you insist on helping, you'll need to leave right now. I'll arrange for a thermocopter to pick you up in one hour. The only question is how this can be done without alerting the entire city."

"Then show me how to get back down to Root Town."

"No. As far as Root Town is concerned, you are in custody. I'm not taking unnecessary risks."

Selest inhaled sharply. "But my friend, Farim—"

"He's safe at the roots."

Selest sighed. "What do you want me to do?"

"Come with me, Doctor."

Once again Selest followed Xenia, this time in the opposite direction and at a much faster pace. A few blocks later, they reached a building with no numbers or markings – just a quiet, nondescript structure nestled between two larger ones.

"This is your exit to the top of the tree," Xenia said, unlocking the heavy door. "There's a platform above. You'll be picked up from there. It won't be an easy climb, but I doubt it will be a problem since you managed the ascent here. You won't have to wait long. Copters are fast."

Selest grasped the door handle but hesitated.

Xenia turned to leave.

"You may be right about education," Selest said, her voice steady. "But fear can't be controlled – just as physical pain can't either. We can only learn how to stop it from controlling us." She looked into lifeless eyes and added, "At least send a doctor to the Root Town. They need one."

Without waiting for a response, she stepped inside and closed the door behind her.

15: The End of Ozhogino

Selest walked through the entrance, expecting the hollow quiet of an abandoned house. Instead, she found herself inside a tree. The outer shell of the massive vertical branch had been carefully preserved, its natural bark concealing what lay within. The core, long since rotted away, had been stripped and smoothed, creating a gradually spiralling tunnel that twisted upwards into darkness. The air inside was thick with the scent of damp wood and faint traces of resin, entering her nostrils like a memory of rain.

She exhaled sharply, gripping the ladder-like notches carved into the walls. Had Xenia sent her up this on purpose? It would have been just as easy to call the thermocopter to a city air dock, but no – this was deliberate. A test. A punishment. Or perhaps just one final reminder of who was in control.

Selest gritted her teeth, adjusted her grip and climbed. The elegant dress she had donned earlier this morning was instantly ruined. The wide-brimmed hat and decorative visor ripped against the walls, forcing her to discard them. The gold and white fabric of the dress caught on the rough inner bark, tearing in places as she struggled higher. Silk and lace were not made for this kind of journey. She swore under her breath.

Step by step, rung by rung, she ascended, her breathing steady but laboured. The tunnel was tight and claustrophobic. Darkness pressed against her, only occasionally interrupted by slits carved into the bark, where beams of pale morning light speared through like silent sentinels. The climb felt endless. Her arms burned, her calves ached, but she refused to stop.

Then, finally, she reached the top.

Selest hauled herself onto the platform, her limbs aching, breath ragged. She felt a little light-headed when she staggered forwards and inhaled sharply as the world expanded before her. The crowns of the colossal trees stretched endlessly in all directions – a metropolis of interwoven branches, platforms and structures suspended high above the ruined Earth. Yet, even this vast network was nothing compared to the sky.

The rising sun painted the horizon in molten metal and amber, its light unfurling across an untouched expanse. Below, the world was still suffocating beneath dense, rust-coloured dust storms – the ever-present consequence of a dying planet. But here, above the Crown, the air was clear. There was no choking haze, no dimmed sunlight, just the boundless sky stretching unbroken.

She caught her breath. Years. It had been years since she had seen the sun like this – unveiled, unfiltered, and very different in size and colour from what people had become accustomed to seeing over the past few millennia. She had almost forgotten its brilliance, the way it burned, the way it touched everything without resistance.

She moved to the edge of the platform and let her legs dangle over the side, momentarily lost in thought. The wind up here was sharper, biting at her exposed skin, but it was clean. It tasted like something long extinct. Like the past you weren't meant to revisit.

Far below, Kiowa's massive trees stood

defiant against the wasteland, rising like ancient sentinels. They were the last remnants of an Earth that had once thrived. The world had collapsed – the Platinum Age reduced to little more than myth, the war between logic and faith consuming all that followed. Humanity had divided. Some embraced the bunkers and thick walls; others fled upward, clinging to the trees like the last vestiges of a dream. But how long before even this refuge crumbled?

Her fingers brushed against something beside her. A folded blanket. A small pack with a water flask tucked inside. Selest frowned and picked up the flask. It was full. Someone had used this place before – perhaps regularly. A waiting point? A meeting place? Or simply a quiet refuge for those who still sought solitude?

She wrapped the blanket around her shoulders and sipped water, letting the silence settle over her like a second skin. The world below was filled with whistles of wind, but everything was almost still up here. It seemed as if the wind lived only in the leaves of the trees, and the creaking of the trunks and branches was nearly therapeutic.

Hours passed. The sun had risen high when the sound came. A low, rhythmic thrum. A vibration in the air, distinct and deliberate.

Selest packed the blanket and flask back into the pack and stood, scanning the horizon. A dark shape emerged against the brightening sky. The thermocopter.

It approached swiftly, a sleek silhouette cutting through the morning air. As it neared, its downdraught whipped through Selest's torn dress, tugging at the loose strands of her black hair. The craft hovered above her, engines pulsing, before a side hatch slid open. A figure leaned out, and a gravitic descent array deployed, its segmented panels extending smoothly, stabilising against the turbulence.

Selest took a steadying breath and

climbed. Her muscles screamed in protest, but she gritted her teeth and forced herself upward. The cold metal rungs bit into her palms, and for a fleeting second, she felt weightless – the vast world stretching below her, dizzying in its distance.

Then strong hands grabbed her arms and hauled her inside.

As she caught her breath, she registered the rows of men and women in dark-armoured uniforms lining the cabin. Space squads. They tried not to stare, but she felt their curiosity. Then she looked up at the figure standing over her.

A young man, his military uniform crisp and precise, dark grey with silver lieutenant insignia on the sleeves.

He sealed the hatch behind her and extended a hand. "Doctor Dvali. My name is Alan Lillypond."

Selest took his hand, gripping it firmly

despite her exhaustion. "I assume you're here to take me to Ozhogino?"

Alan nodded, stepping back as the thermocopter banked. "Apologies for your long wait, but I have hot herbal tea for you. And bad news for all of us."

Selest dusted off her ruined dress, rolling her shoulders. "The tea first, then. Thank you, Lieutenant."

Lieutenant Alan Lillypond gestured towards a small compartment near the cockpit, where a thermal canister was strapped into place. He poured her a cup as the craft surged forwards.

She took a cautious sip, letting the warmth spread through her. Alan crossed his arms, studying her. "We're heading straight to the resort, and we'll be joining the others soon – but it might not be enough. The Cruisers are moving faster than we expected. They are already inside."

Selest lowered the plastic cup. "How long until we arrive?"

"Two hours. Maybe less if we push it." He tilted his head slightly, taking in her dishevelled state. "Doctor, you look like hell, by the way."

She smirked tiredly. "Spent the morning climbing through a tree. No time for beauty sleep."

Alan chuckled, shaking his head. "I can offer you a change of clothes. I don't doubt even military gear would suit you well."

Selest let the compliment pass, leaning against the wall, watching as the sky stretched beyond the glass. "Thank you. It'll do for now."

Alan sat across from her, his expression turning serious. "Mr Veir was preparing for the worst, but he does not have that many men. If Ozhogino falls, we lose everything you worked for at the Eternum Project. We can't let that happen."

Selest tightened her grip on the cup.

Their vessel moved fast, slicing through the sky, carrying them towards the north-west – towards the resort, war and a future neither could predict.

She didn't know whose uniform she'd been given, only that it was made for a female scout with more muscle and a flatter chest. Still, Selest was grateful for the warmth and comfort – it allowed her body to stop shaking and finally relax. She even managed a nap, curled tightly on the narrow seat in the corner.

When she opened her eyes, the tundra stretched endlessly beneath the thermocopter, a vast expanse of ice and rock broke only by the occasional frozen river winding like a dead vein through the permafrost. Selest sat near the open side door, the wind biting through the fabric of her grey uniform as she watched the ground blur past below. The sun hung low on the horizon, an indifferent eye over the wasteland.

Three more thermocopters flanked them in a tight formation, their dark hulls slicing through the sky with brutal efficiency. The troopers inside them were silent, their weapons ready and their faces unreadable behind their visors.

Lieutenant Alan Lillypond stood near the cockpit and spoke into his communicator, his voice clipped and professional.

"We're three minutes out. No signals from the surface. Whatever's happening, we're stepping into a blackout."

Selest's fingers tightened on the strap across her chest. Ozhogino had been under attack when the first distress calls were sent, and now silence had swallowed everything. She forced herself to breathe, steeling herself for what they might find.

As they crested the final ridge, the remains of Ozhogino came into view.

The entrance to the underground

complex had been exposed, its once-sealed surface doors blown apart. Scattered bodies lay around the opening, their figures twisted and lifeless. Some in the resort guard's uniform and some in sky-blue robes. Selest breathed a sigh of relief because these bodies did not include corpses wearing the green overalls of the young Loaders and the white jumpsuits of the medical workers and teachers.

But perhaps she would see them in the underground corridors of these vast facilities.

It was too early to stop worrying. Fires flickered in the ruins of outbuildings, casting long, wavering shadows. The ground was littered with debris – shattered drones, abandoned weapons and blood frozen into black stains against the ice.

Alan's voice crackled through the comms. "Deploy. Now."

The thermocopters descended swiftly, sending up whirling clouds of ice and ash as the troopers dropped into the chaos below. Gunfire still echoed from deeper within the facility, but it was clear that the main slaughter had already taken place.

Selest leaped from the thermocopter, her boots crunching against the icy ground. Her breath came in sharp gasps as she scanned for familiar faces through the wreckage. She found them. Too many of them.

Rokhel lay sprawled near the entrance, her body half-covered in frost, her wide eyes frozen in a final expression of horror. Paul Anev lay motionless a few steps away, his fingers still curled around a useless medical case. Selest stumbled back, a strangled sound escaping her throat.

But there was no sign of Gleb or other Loaders.

"Doctor!" Alan's voice cut through the chaos. "The lift's operational. We're heading down."

She looked away from the bodies and followed him, her heart hammering. The underground corridors of Ozhogino were eerily silent. Power flickered in and out, leaving stretches of the passageways in near-total darkness. The walls were smeared with blood, the aftermath of desperate fighting. But there were no more enemies here. Only the dead.

"I don't understand. If the guards failed to protect the resort and all fell on the surface, who killed these Cruisers? The rest of the staff were no combatants; they are dead too," Alan said, signalling his men to check all the premises.

"I am not sure, but I think . . . Lieutenant, I want to check on the boss first. He might be hiding children in his rooms," Selest said, leading the way to Dominic's quarters.

There were a few dead Cruisers before the door, but still no sign of Loaders.

Selest pushed open the door and froze.

Fred Shademaker was slumped, barely conscious, in the corner, his hands bound behind his back. Standing over him was Professor Mel Sancho. Her wild, grey-streaked hair hung in tangled waves around her face, her once-pristine lab coat smeared with grime. Mel clutched an old scalpel in her trembling hands – a museum piece from Veir's collection – and muttered feverishly under her breath.

"Above gods . . . must hold power above gods . . . they won't take it . . . can't take it . . ."

Selest stepped forwards cautiously. "Mel, put the scalpel down."

Sancho's eyes flicked to her, unfocused and shining with madness. "Doctor Dvali . . . you left. You abandoned the work and left it to rot . . . but I remained. I remained!"

Mel Sancho lunged, but Alan was faster. He grabbed her wrist, twisting the weapon from her grasp before she could strike. The old woman let out a choked sob, collapsing to her knees, still whispering to herself.

Selest rushed to Fred, untying his hands with quick, practised movements. "Are you hurt?"

Fred shook his head, his eyes weary but alert. "No. Just . . . tired of listening to her."

Selest forced a thin, humourless sniff, then straightened. "Genatsvale, I haven't seen any children yet – dead or alive. Where is Dominic?"

Fred Shademaker exhaled, the lines on his face deepening. "They're here. All of them. They're wearing my bio-suits, but you won't find them. They'll find you – when it's safe." His voice faltered. "I don't know about Dominic. Unfortunately, all our colleagues . . . Oh, Selest . . ."

"I know." The grief lodged in her throat, but she forced herself to stay steady. "I'm so sorry, Fred."

She pulled him into a brief embrace

before turning to Alan. "Lieutenant, please have your men take care of these two. Just be cautious with the woman. She might be ... unpredictable."

Alan nodded, his expression cold. "We'll handle it, but the priority —"

"Yes, yes," Selest interrupted. "You want to make sure the Loaders are safe. Trust me. I'll find them. I know where to look next."

She made her way towards the library, Alan and a few of his men following closely behind. The library had always been a maze – a place of retreat, of learning, of play. Even as children, the Loaders had mastered its labyrinthine corridors, playing hide and seek among the tall shelved bookcases and in its depths as soon as they learned to read.

As the small group approached the doors, one of the troopers stepped in front of them, holding a compact device with thin cords branching from its casing, snaking towards the walls. The screen projected a grainy, monochrome image of the library interior – stacks, furniture and a single bright silhouette moving between the aisles.

"What is that?" Selest asked, narrowing her eyes at the device.

"Xyntha Relayer," Alan answered. "A new military-grade multi-spectrum scanning tool."

"What does it do?"

"It scans and analyses the space behind walls, mapping structural details, energy signatures and organic movement. It reconstructs activity in real time using infrared displacement mapping using quantum echo data, displaying holographic projections of people and their actions on a built-in screen. Watch closely."

Selest peered at the projection. The figure on the screen, draped in a long robe, moved with uncertainty, as if lost.

The young trooper operating the device spoke in a hushed tone. "These guys came to hunt the Loaders, but it looks like they're the ones being hunted." He tapped the screen, adjusting the resolution. "That's the last Cruiser still standing. The rest are piled up near the door."

Selest leaned in, studying the monochrome display. She saw another figure whose moves were unnerving – inhumanly smooth, calculated. Every motion was controlled, and every shift of weight was optimised for balance and speed. She could almost sense the silent, efficient footfalls of a body engineered beyond human limits.

Then, on the periphery of the screen, another shape emerged. A flicker of movement too fast to register fully.

The trooper stiffened. "There. Did you see that?"

Alan nodded grimly. "They're toying

with him."

Selest exhaled with relief, recognising the tactics. The Loaders had always been fast, but now they moved with the coordination of a hunting pack. They did not need to rush into reckless attacks. Instead, they stalked their prey, manipulating its path, forcing it towards its inevitable conclusion.

The man in the robe hesitated, then sprinted towards the exit.

Instantly, numerous shapes dropped from the bookshelves above, landing in absolute silence. The robed figure twisted, then tried to bolt in another direction, but half a dozen Loaders stepped into his path.

Selest felt a sharp pang of unease.

"I need to go in," she said, stepping towards the door.

Alan caught her wrist. "Doctor, surely they won't kill him."

She looked up at him, her jaw set. "I'm

afraid they might."

She pushed the door but was too late.

They stopped. Two of them lowered the motionless man on the floor and all turned towards her. All the Loaders were dressed in identical dark-green overalls, hiding the enhanced bio-suits that have become their second skin. Selest kneeled beside the six figures in blue robes slumped against the wall. A quick assessment told her they were alive, just unconscious. The Loaders had struck precisely – targeting vital points to disable, not kill. Their attacks were designed, efficient. As for the Cruisers? They were trained, undoubtedly, but likely driven by the desperation of withdrawal.

Selest rose to her feet, scanned the group and counted them.

She had grown used to how Loaders behaved – unlike normal teenagers. They didn't chatter, ask unnecessary questions, share anxious glances or exchange remarks. They acknowledged her instructions and moved in seamless coordination, following the paratroopers without hesitation.

She reached out, catching one of them by the wrist. "Victor."

The boy turned to face her, his sharp eyes calm. He turned and took her fingers in both hands – not unkindly, but without warmth.

"There are only forty-five of you here," Selest said, her voice steady but urgent. "Where are the other three? Where is Mr Veir?"

Victor held her gaze for a second. "One of us was killed. By the men in blue robes."

Selest felt a cold weight settle in her chest. "Killed?" Her throat tightened. "Who? Gleb?"

Victor shook his head. "No. Gleb hasn't been weaker or slower than us."

That was true. Whatever remained of the fragile boy she once knew was long gone.

"Then who?"

"It was Max," Victor continued. "He was too close to the entrance when they attacked. He didn't make it."

Selest's breath hitched. "Where is he?"

"Still lying under the table in the cafeteria."

A promise formed on her lips; then she realised she was already crying. "I won't leave him behind."

Victor gave the smallest nod of gratitude. "We're all glad you're back, Doctor Dvali." He squeezed her fingers gently once more, then released her and hurried to rejoin the others.

"Wait! Did you kill all those Cruisers in the corridors?"

The boy, still running, spun around to answer. "No. It was Mr Veir. He did all of it alone."

And then he was gone.

Selest wiped her face, steadying her breath. There was no time for grief. Not now.

Forty-five accounted for. One dead. Two missing.

Where were they? And where was the first Loader who could kill many Cruisers single-handedly?

Alan turned to his men, his voice sharp and decisive. "We need to sweep the entire resort. Every corridor, every chamber, every sealed-off section. If they're alive, we'll find them." He glanced at Selest. "Doctor Dvali, are you ready to join those kids on the surface?"

"Soon," she said. "I need to retrieve something first."

She turned away, her feet carrying her towards a place she had never expected to return to.

The corridors leading to her special quarters were undisturbed, thick with silence. It had been their sanctuary – hers and Aldo's – buried deep within an abandoned wing no one had reason to check. She had not stepped over its threshold since the day they left the resort together for the last time.

And now she was returning alone.

Her fingers trembled slightly as she touched the lock panel. The door released with a quiet hiss.

The air inside was still. Undisturbed.

Yet something felt wrong.

Selest stepped inside. The apartment was exactly as they had left it – the neatly arranged books on the low shelf, the blanket draped over the worn-out sofa, the mug Aldo had left on the side table. Even the ring still sat untouched on the windowsill.

It was all the same.

Except it wasn't.

Her heart pounded as she took another step forwards – then stopped, her breath catching in her throat.

The bedroom door. Something was off.

Selest wasn't a Loader, but over the

years, she had learned to listen. To notice.

A sound – so faint she almost missed it. A breath.

Someone was there. Standing just behind the door, perhaps mere centimetres away.

Waiting.

16: Veir's Will

Selest's bedroom door opened inwards. She took a step back and drove her boot into it with all her strength. It slammed against the wall and bounced slightly. She saw a figure jump back in the dim red glow of the emergency lights.

"Ah, it *is* you," said a familiar voice, smooth as ever. "I've been hoping for this scenario."

Sister Maria stood upright in a mazarine-blue robe, her expression composed, though her eyes glittered from the drug. Selest hadn't expected the cramped bedroom to be so full.

On the bed lay Dominic, half of his face bloodied, but he was still breathing. At the head of the bed, bound back-to-back with synthetic rope, sat Gleb and Karagoz. Both teens held themselves rigid, alert. Two men in sky-blue robes flanked them, weapons trained, while Maria pointed a scavenged zapper squarely at Selest.

"You seem quite at home here now," Maria said, her voice almost conversational. "You've got yourself a new set of quarters. I'm grateful – these kids watered my lime tree."

She pointed at the large potted plant in the corner.

"It's not yours," Selest said flatly. "It belonged to my best friend."

Maria's smile faltered. Her tone turned sharp. "Aren't you curious why we're all here?"

Selest scanned the room. "It's not difficult to work out. You underestimated the Loaders and realised your mission was a failure. You lost. A single Loader was worth more than your entire sect. And now he's injured. You found this hidden place through the boy. If I hadn't returned, you would've disappeared quietly after the evacuation. You needed hostages – and now you've got one more."

Maria gave a short laugh. "You were always clever, Sel, but never wise. If you'd joined me, none of this would've been necessary. How many of you are here? Who will come looking for you? If no one offers safe passage, I'll kill these two skinheads first. Then you. Dominic is already a dead man."

Selest's eyes flicked to the bed. Blood seeped through Dominic's shirt, his chest rising and falling in shallow, wheezing gasps. A collapsed lung, perhaps worse. Yet even in pain, he wore the faint trace of a smile as if amused by something only he could see.

The young couple on the floor were watching her.

"He told us not to resist, Doctor Dvali," Gleb said, his voice steady. "We're following Mr Veir's orders. As long as he's alive."

Selest turned back to Maria. "Looks like killing him isn't in your interest. Unless you truly think your escape is guaranteed – by your Lord."

Maria's grip on the zapper tightened.

"Faith has always been humanity's fiercest force. Your world fell because you turned away from it – trusting your machines, your science, believing they'd make you gods. But you put too much confidence in yourselves. Reason taught you independence, not unity. It severed the old bonds. Faith ... faith binds. It gives people something to lean on – together. It was never a weakness. It was the spine of our race."

"Faith leads to blind obedience," Selest countered. "It lets you kill in the name of something unprovable. We seek truth, not dominion."

Maria tilted her head, considering. Then she sighed. "You always sounded like a scientist. Even now, facing death, you still preach your gospel of logic."

"Gods didn't build that gun you are holding," Selest said. "Yet you use it instead of a crucifix."

Maria's lips pressed into a line.

Dominic stirred, his voice barely a whisper. "Sister Maria . . . a request."

She turned, cautious. "What do you want?"

"Before you do what you believe must be done . . . grant me one last act of mercy. Let me bless these two."

Selest stiffened, not believing her ears. "What?"

Maria's eyes narrowed. "A blessing?"

"They are young," Dominic said. "If they must die, let them die in grace."

For a long moment, Maria hesitated. Then she gave a single nod.

"Bow your heads," she ordered.

The boy and the girl shifted awkwardly, lowering their heads as much as the rope allowed. Dominic reached out with a trembling hand, placing his fingers gently on their foreheads, one after the other.

For a few seconds, all was still.

Then everything exploded.

Karagoz twisted, snapping the rope like a paper ribbon. Gleb moved in a blur, seizing the arms of the two armed men before they could fire. Weapons clattered to the floor. In a single breath, their captors were disarmed and unconscious.

Maria barely reacted in time – but Gleb was faster. Her zapper was ripped from her grasp and activated in less than a second.

Dominic's head dropped on one side. A perfect hole burned through his chest. His body slumped onto the bed, lifeless.

Selest gasped. "No . . ."

Maria reeled, her eyes wide in disbelief. "You . . . you shot him!"

Gleb lowered the weapon. "He gave me the order."

Selest rushed to the bed, gripping Dominic's hand. It was still warm. A soft smile lingered on his lips.

Maria's fury ignited. "Blasphemy," she hissed, her hand trembling as it slipped inside her robe. But instead of drawing a weapon, she bit down hard on a large green capsule. Calmly, almost reverently, she sank to the floor beside the lime plant. "Now my only escape is to your realm, my Lord," she whispered, closing her eyes, "Take me . . . as I am and . . ."

But the final words never came.

Selest hardly watched her dying. She looked at Dominic. His death had been purposeful – a final act of control.

She turned to Gleb. "You said he gave you the order. How? Was it a signal?"

Gleb shook his head. "No. It was a data transfer – his final protocol, triggered by physical contact. His design. He uploaded the message, the data and his last decision."

"Now you'll carry on his work," Karagoz added, her voice quiet and steady. "Under our guidance."

She spoke with unnerving composure, as if the two of them hadn't just taken a life, as if this were nothing more than a passing of roles in a carefully prepared plan.

Selest realised just how much had changed at the resort – how much she'd missed.

Dominic didn't just believe in the Loaders. He knew what they could become – far more than anyone ever dared to imagine.

She swallowed hard. "I suppose I should be surprised. But today I've seen just how far ahead you are – in skill, in knowledge . . . and in ethics too."

She let go of Dominic's hand, her voice softening.

"If Loaders can preserve what's left of humanity, then I'll do what I can to help them. I promise."

Dominic Veir lay still, his smile frozen in peace.

Soon, the apartment – and the entire resort – emptied in a slow, solemn procession. The brief battle had left its mark, the scent of death, blood and burned plastic lingering in the corridors and halls.

Alan's men worked in silence, their boots thudding against bloodstained floors as they packed the Cruisers' corpses into thick burial bags and dragged them away. The medical officers moved quietly, their faces concealed behind protective masks. They checked Selest's vitals, then turned to the teenagers, their gloved hands tracing over Karagoz and Gleb's bodies, searching for injuries and marvelling at bio-suits they'd never seen before.

Satisfied, they carefully lifted Dominic's body onto a stretcher. Once filled with purpose and relentless drive, his frame now lay limp and drained. Half his face remained streaked with drying blood, a stark contrast to the pallor of his skin.

Selest's thoughts fastened. Dominic hadn't been one of her creations. For the last thirty years, he had modified himself – upgrading, innovating and evolving. Every part of him held knowledge, data and secrets. Even in death, he was invaluable.

She stepped closer as officers secured him for transport. "Please make sure he's taken to a Resistance-controlled morgue," she said firmly. "Him, and the boy who died in the canteen. I want both of them stored properly. It's critical that no one touches them until I arrive. Please. Do you understand?"

The lead officer hesitated only for a moment, then nodded.

"Understood, Doctor. What about the guards and your colleagues? Do they have families we should contact?"

"Perhaps. But those families assumed them dead long ago. I'll show you the cremation chambers," Selest answered, feeling a sting of memories of how they used those chambers just a few years ago.

Beside her, Karagoz gently took Gleb's arm. "Come on. Let's get out of here. We need to join the rest."

Her voice had softened, coaxing. But Gleb remained rooted to the spot, eyes fixed on Selest.

"You don't need to worry about your Eternum data," he said. "We have it all. Stored safely. Mr Veir's orders."

Selest raised an eyebrow. "Of course you do. I thought as much." She rested a hand on his shoulder. "Go on. I'll join you when it's time."

Reluctantly, Gleb let Karagoz pull him away, glancing back only once before disappearing down the corridor.

Selest stepped into the wardrobe, changed from the borrowed military gear into her own travel clothes, and lingered, caught in a pause she couldn't quite explain. Leaving this apartment the second time felt different. Her gaze drifted across her sanctuary, hidden deep within the vast residential section of the resort. Every surface held echoes of her years in

Ozhogino: relentless research, habitual solitude and the quiet war against inevitability.

The bed where Aldo used to sleep, his limbs spread like a starfish. The terminal where she'd once pored over medical reports. A single shelf, still lined with small, priceless artefacts from another life. Everything remained familiar – none of it had ever truly become home, despite Aldo's efforts. Not yet, anyway.

A dull ache settled in her chest.

She closed her eyes and let herself remember his laughter, hands and the rare way he could steady her when her strength faltered. He had been her anchor, the one who'd made the burden of knowledge bearable. *He* was her home here, not these rooms.

Selest's eyes landed on the fake windowsill – digital light still glowing faintly. Aldo's proposal ring still rested there. She picked it up and slipped it into her pocket. A small part of him, to carry forwards with the other relics of those she had lost.

In the bedroom corner, Lia, the lime tree, waited – its delicate leaves reaching for a dim glow. The last reminder of another lost friend. Long gone.

Selest took the pot gently in her arms.

By the time the cremation arrangements were complete, every corpse – Cruiser or resort dweller – had been wrapped in the same grey space-burial bags. Selest had never seen them before, but she'd heard the space navy and orbital station dwellers used them. Highly flammable materials turned their contents into a flash of sparks when released into the atmosphere – bright, silent and gone in seconds.

They packed one hundred and eighty bodies. But there weren't enough bags. Dozens of the dead Cruisers were burned without them.

Selest couldn't tell which bags held enemies and which held friends – Rokhel, Paul, even Maria – though she preferred to remember her as Abeni.

How strange, she thought, watching the loading crews. *Death makes everyone the same.*

At the lift, a commotion stirred. An aged voice, hoarse with urgency, called out to Selest.

"Doctor Dvali! Selest!"

Fred Shademaker pushed past Alan's men, his frail form trembling with the effort.

"I need a word. Now."

Lieutenant Lillypond took the pot from Selest and gestured for his soldiers to let the old man through. "Make it quick. We are leaving soon."

Fred gripped Selest's arm, his fingers surprisingly strong.

"Come with me. There's something you must take away from this place."

She followed him through winding, half-lit corridors. The halls felt eerily empty now –

ghosts in their absence. They stopped at her old lab.

The door creaked open.

Inside lay what had once been the heart of her work: creation, experiments, breakthroughs. Now it was a graveyard.

The artificial wombs stood like silent sentinels, their chambers empty. Hundreds of them. Lifeless.

A spike of dread shot through her. Why are they here? Was one still in use? Had someone been left behind? Unformed, unborn?

But Fred was already moving, leading her to a frozen storage unit once used for preserving gametes and zygotes. She remembered it being cleared. Completely.

He bent down, hands shaking slightly, and withdrew a silver container no larger than a thermal flask.

There was a name etched on the side.

Rebekah.

Selest's breath caught.

"This is Gleb's sister," Fred said. "Paul and Rokhel asked me to preserve her. We didn't know when you'd return, and they didn't trust Sancho. It's just a morula. But I slowed the division. You'll know what to do."

Selest ran her fingers across the engraved letters.

"This container . . . it works like your bio-suits, doesn't it?"

Fred nodded. "She'll survive – for a while. But if you leave her here, she'll die."

It wasn't just a frozen embryo, but the new responsibility felt like a ton of iron. This was a legacy – the last hope of a family wiped out. Friends who had trusted her with their son . . . and now this.

She closed her hand around the container.

"There's no question. I'll take Rebekah," Selest said. "I'll keep her safe, Genatsvale. Give her a chance to be a normal human, just like her mother wanted, I assume."

Fred exhaled, the relief plain in his tired eyes.

"Good. I was hoping you'd say that."

As Selest cradled the container to her chest, something shifted deep within her – an unspoken promise – a new commitment, her reason to go on. She even felt a little lighter and more hopeful.

She wasn't just leaving the resort. She was leaving behind an era. A world. A version of herself that was so hard to find at the start.

And ahead? There was something new once again. Uncertain. Fragile. But worth saving.

With one last glance at the abandoned lab, Selest turned and walked away.

17: The Tree House

Selest opened her eyes to the filtered light of morning, then stretched slowly beneath the soft quilt.

The ceiling above her was a curved panel of living wood, braided with old copper veins and sensor threads. Her room was nestled within the massive trunk of a giant oak tree in the heart of Wales. The facility in its crown was called the Tree House. It, too, had been designed decades ago by Dominic Veir – one of his earliest projects, she recalled, from the time before the Kiowa City or Two Tree market in her home town, before the war turned scientists into tacticians.

She sat up slowly, letting the scent of fresh coffee drift into her senses. No one had made it for her – the machine in the standard-issue kitchen unit handled that, and a compact assembly of ZPE fridge, boiler and oven was programmed for quiet efficiency. The air in the Tree House was still thick with a deliberate peace. Selest paused, allowing herself to think of Dominic again, and offered him silent gratitude.

Her new quarters were modest. Nothing like the quarters in Ozhogino's Resort of Hope. But comfort lived in the details. The desk's base had been hand-carved from the tree itself, and thick glass covered the real windows – offering a view of a genuine horizon where dust storms rolled over distant hills and real stars were visible most nights. Lia, her lime tree, now sat proudly by the windowsill, basking in honest sunlight for the first time in years and blossoming for the first time ever. On the nearby shelf, her small collection of artefacts had been arranged with care: a scrap of turquoise velvet – rescued during the evacuation and all that remained of her mother's dress, her father's piece of weathered slate, her old gold medal, a black pendant, and Aldo's ring. Each was a relic of someone lost, a fragment of a life scattered by time. Her music collection, sadly, had not survived.

Just as her life before Ozhogino was long gone, the resort itself had vanished, too, on that same tragic day.

The blast wasn't loud.

They had already left the resort, their transport skimming the line of clouds, when it happened. No one said a word at first. The air inside the cabin had shifted, a strange pressure rippling through the walls – a shiver in the fabric of the world – something ancient and wrong.

It wasn't the Resistance, Alan had confirmed that much.

He didn't know who had triggered the detonation, but he suspected infiltration. Though several Cruiser prisoners had been disarmed and taken into custody, one might have escaped arrest and either died with the resort or left with them all, concealed among the evacuees. The medics wore masks, making it easy for someone to slip in unseen.

Selest shuddered. The idea that a Cruiser could've examined her . . . or touched the young Loaders . . . it made her stomach turn. Nevertheless, the Loaders assured her they would have detected an irregular heartbeat or any unusual substances in anyone who came close enough. Upon arrival, she'd insisted on seeing the prisoners, but the tall black-haired man she feared wasn't among them. None of

Alan's soldiers recalled picking up a body that matched her description of Father Sebastian. And yet, one of the captives admitted he had been part of the raid. The priest had brought the bomb, calling it "the holy flame to destroy the nest of abominations."

He was there. And then he disappeared.

The medical team recalled an old woman – Sancho – clinging tightly to a tall man in a resort uniform, someone who appeared deeply concerned for her. No one had recognised him as a threat; everyone was too busy to double-check. Fred Shademaker, who had kept his distance from "Crazy Mel" during the evacuation, later insisted that there were no other survivors. Needless to say – once they landed in Wales, the tall man vanished. No one could tell where and how, not even Mel Sancho.

He had travelled in the same vessel as Selest and the Loaders. That, she realised with a grim clarity, might have been the only reason they were safe.

No one saw the priest again.

Selest rose, brushing sleep from her eyes, and walked to her desk. She made herself a latte. As she lifted the mug, the holo-screen blinked to life with a pulsing message from Lieutenant Commander Lillypond.

She tapped it. Alan's image flickered into view – tired but alert.

"I'm sorry, Doctor," he said without preamble. "My people went back to Ozhogino. There's nothing retrievable left. Everything is buried deeper than after that Canadian quake."

Selest nodded grimly. The most complete library on Earth was lost.

"But," he continued, "we can get you at least a few artificial wombs from another resort of hope. More refrigeration units too. Might take a few days."

"Thank you, Alan. Please, hurry. I need them as soon as possible."

He hesitated, then asked, "Are you truly restarting Veir's Eternum Project? You know I've got new squads forming, and those teenagers you brought back . . . they're under a protection programme. We can't use them yet."

Selest's voice sharpened. "You mean you *don't know how* to use them yet. Do you think we have time? You told me yourself – no one at Central Command can tell you how many sects exist or the real size of their congregations. They're growing while we argue."

Alan exhaled, rubbing his temple. "We're stretched thin. We're fighting more than zealots now – we're fighting their allies. Collaborators who know how our systems work. People we once relied on. Plus, we are trying to find the source of that drug you described."

"Then train my boys and girls," she snapped. "I know you don't trust them – maybe you're even afraid. But trust *me*. They're good.

Better than us . . . in every way that matters. I mean it – in every way that is good. The good guys, as you'd say."

Selest paused. Because even now, after everything, she still didn't fully understand the values the Loaders held.

She remembered the cremation at the resort, the thick black smoke curling into the clouds from the chimney, just its tip protruding from the ground above. Gleb and Karagoz stood with the others, silent and composed, waiting for the command to board the vessel. Selest had approached them gently, uncertainly – perhaps hoping to offer a human ritual as comfort.

"Would you like to say goodbye?" she asked. "To your sibling Max. To Mr Veir. Their bodies have been transferred to the thermocopter. We can hold a ceremony. Something simple."

But not a single Loader flinched. They simply looked at her – not unkindly, but with calm surprise. As though she had offered them something they could no longer perceive.

Even Gleb – who had lost both of his parents that day – appeared unmoved. His mother and father, both human, had died shielding others in the assault. And yet he only gave her a soft shake of the head, then spoke a phrase that had haunted her ever since.

"A sad but negligible loss. Less than one point four per cent of the shared data. What we have is sufficient."

That was all. No need for farewell.

She had nodded then, unsure what else to do – but the words lingered long after the fire had died. And now, in the quiet of the Tree House, they returned to her again.

The Loaders were not children. Not any more. They were becoming something else – part human, part architecture. A product of her effort and the effort of those now gone. A community with its own language for loss. A logic she could record, observe, try to understand – but not share.

And yet . . . he had used the word *sad*.

And she wasn't sure what was more painful: that they didn't grieve, didn't need to, or that they grieved in a way she would never know.

She leaned forwards, her voice firm but pleading. "Alan! Please! Help me finish what Veir started. Fred's managed to track down one of his former students, but it's not enough. We need more – scientists, medics, people who believe in something more than mere survival."

Alan's voice softened. "I'll send what I can. However, after this, the navy's involvement is limited. I have my orders. We'll protect your Tree House, but the rest is yours to sort out, Doctor."

His image blinked out.

Selest sat back in her chair, fingers tapping against her ceramic mug. The morning sun slanted across the room, catching the edge of the lime tree's pot.

She got up, walked towards the kitchen unit, opened the fridge and reached for the small silver container.

Rebekah was the name on the smooth metal, the letters crisp and solemn.

A few cells, slowed in development by Fred's clever craft. The child her friends had entrusted to her. And now, perhaps, the last result of the incredible projects.

Selest lifted the container gently, holding it to her hot temple. It was cold – colder than needed – not like it should be able to hold something alive.

"This time," she whispered, "we do it right."

She placed it back in the fridge, returned to her desk and opened a new holo-tab. Fred's former student, Maiser, had already drafted a proposal: names of biologists, geneticists and engineers. People scattered across the archipelagos and safe zones, waiting to be called. She reviewed them with the precision of a surgeon and the weariness of a woman who'd lost too much.

There were knocks at her door later that day – Karagoz, quiet and somehow taller.

"Doctor Selest, there's a woman on the tree to see you," the girl said. "She says she's your friend."

Selest's back stiffened at those words.

"I thought I lost all my old friends."

"She doesn't look old. She brought you some kind of painting as a gift and said her name was Kaelin. She's from Kiowa Resistance Hide."

The name settled like a weight in Selest's chest. Kaelin. Eldrin's granddaughter. The one who had left her stranded on the great tree in Kiowa, when every second had mattered. She stood, smoothing the front of her shirt and brushing stray strands of hair – no longer so black – from her face.

"Let her in," she said.

Kaelin entered with the same quiet strength Selest remembered. Her golden curls were gathered in a loose braid, and her eyes were luminous with something beyond joy – something like purpose. She carried a canvas wrapped in cloth with both hands, careful and reverent.

"I hope I'm not intruding," Kaelin said softly, stepping inside.

"You are welcome here," Selest replied, but her voice held a guarded note.

Kaelin nodded once, then hesitated. "I simply had to come in person," she said, lowering the painting slightly. "To apologise. For running away back then."

Selest folded her arms. "You panicked."

"No, Doctor. I don't panic." Her tone was calm – determined. "I did something nasty. I understand that now. I left you on purpose. I was jealous and wanted Farim to be mine alone." She looked down, ashamed. "And it was in vain. He later said you weren't together."

"He was right," Selest said evenly.

"Well, there you go." Kaelin gave a humourless smile. "But it was still wrong. Nasty, as I said. Because I thought you would be captured. Now everything is different. We know about the Resistance in Crown City – they've opened their hospitals and schools for us. But we still prefer to live among the roots. We take the elevator up to the shops – we work and study there." She paused, her voice humbled. "Please. Forgive me."

Selest studied her for a long moment. Kaelin stood her ground. A survivor, still very young, yet someone hardened by the world. But not entirely. The honesty in her words, the effort to make things right – it counted for something.

Selest nodded. "I forgive you."

Kaelin's eyes lit up with quiet relief. She stepped forwards and, without thinking, gave Selest a brief but heartfelt hug.

Then she unwrapped the bundle in her hands and turned it around.

The portrait hit Selest like a shockwave.

Farim – her steady companion in peril, whose face and body had been ravaged by fire, whose scars told a history of cruelty and survival, stood tall and whole in Eldrin's painting. The scars were still there but reworked. The fire had not erased his features – it had become part of it. In the portrait, he looked like a being from another world. A warrior, perhaps. A sentinel.

His single eye. That was what stilled her breath. Eldrin added some colour to the reconstructed iris. There was pain there, yes, but beneath it, something familiar. A silent resilience. Depth. The kind of soul you only encounter once in a lifetime. He looked like someone else Selest once knew.

"Your grand-grandfather ... he made him look better," she said, her voice barely a whisper.

Kaelin tilted her head. "He painted exactly what he saw. And what I saw. He painted many portraits of Farim and both of us."

She hesitated, then smiled with a quiet boldness.

"Farim and I are getting married. I'd like you to come to Great Elm and celebrate with us. He couldn't come with me today – he's building us a house – but he wanted you to have the painting and this." She reached into her satchel and pulled out a small data device. "He recorded something for you."

Selest accepted it with cold fingers, plugged it into her holo-screen, and pressed play.

Farim's face appeared alive and smiling.

He spoke with a lightness Selest hadn't heard in his voice. He thanked her and told her he no longer felt like a freak. These people – Kaelin, Eldrin, the others – had given him back something he thought he'd lost forever: a sense of belonging. A home. Love.

"I can be myself again," he said, smiling as though it still surprised him. "Thank you, Doctor Dvali. For saving me and giving me the chance to live like this."

And then, just as the recording was about to end, he looked away, as if distracted by something off-screen, and said, "Bye, Lesty. I hope to see you soon."

Selest froze.

She rewound it. Played it again. And again. There was no doubt. His voice, his cadence, the nickname only one man had ever spoken.

Lesty.

She let out a breath she hadn't known she

was holding.

Of course it was him. He had been there – all this time. Alive. Pretending to be his own pilot to shield her from more grief, as soon as he realised what had happened to him.

Her Aldo.

She sank into her chair, her chest tightening with the load of knowing. Found and lost. Again. Was this the third time? The fourth? And this time, it was an act of love.

Kaelin moved to speak but stopped when she saw the look on Selest's face.

"I can't go to your wedding," Selest said at last, her voice distant. "Too much work."

She stood, crossed the room to the shelf where her most precious relics lay, and picked up the beautiful platinum band with a spark of ruby on it.

Aldo's ring.

She returned and placed it gently in Kaelin's hand.

"Please," she said. "Keep this. It belonged to my fiancé. Farim knew him well. He died in the same fire. I think it will make a perfect wedding ring for you."

Kaelin blinked in surprise. "But why? And why wouldn't you come? Farim won't believe it —"

Selest's smile was warm. "Trust me. He will. He is a good man. Very understanding."

Kaelin held the ring to her chest with a silent vow in her eyes. Then she turned to leave, pausing only to say, "You are a good friend, you know. Farim always said that."

Selest didn't answer. She watched as Kaelin disappeared down the corridor, leaving her alone again. Not quite broken. But reshaped.

She turned off the holo-screen and faced the window.

Outside, the wind swept through the high branches of the Tree House, carrying whispers of old ghosts.

She would not see Aldo again – not now. Her path still wound forwards, with the fragile trust of the Loaders under her care.

But one day . . . from a safe distance.

Maybe.

For now, she would try to stop this feeling from taking control of her.

Selest whispered his name – just once, like a fading song. Then she turned back to her terminal and began again.

To be continued.

Trailer for V2 – When Platinum Rusts: Ipsum

Vatslav Maiser had never been more aware of his heartbeat than when the lights flickered in the medical chamber. Not from worry — though that was always there, lurking — but because of the tension in the air. It pressed against the polymer walls, disturbed only by the slow rhythm of eighteen active artificial wombs. Eighteen silent beginnings.

He adjusted the light on his wristband and glanced at the narrow cot where Rebekah Anev lay curled like a kitten, her fine hair damp with baby sweat. Just one year old and already a bundle of sorrow wrapped in impossible code. A normal child — not of design, but of love, yes — yet also born of irretrievable losses.

Next to her stood Selest Dvali, eyes fixed on the monitoring panel. Almost forty-four, though her face had aged well beyond that — lines etched by compromise and a lifetime of unrest. She moved with the controlled precision of someone who didn't have energy to waste. He had never known a woman so brilliant. Or so alone.

She stood by the screens, hands folded behind her back, and watched the readouts scroll past as if they belonged to someone else.

This is wrong, she told him a thousand times. *This should not exist.*

And yet it did.

That was the part no one prepared you for — not the horror, not the guilt, but the endurance of it. Wrongness that didn't collapse under being named. Something that kept running, humming, producing data and heartbeats and tomorrow.

If she left, someone else would take her place, sent by the Resistance. Someone braver, perhaps. Or wiser. Someone who would not flinch at the numbers, who would see only efficiency where Selest still saw faces. The project would not stop out of shame. It would only grow quieter.

Maiser felt the prick of pity.

"She won't save the world," he thought. "But she won't abandon it either. And I won't abandon her."

It was not a justification. Maiser knew that.

It was a comment to share the moral burden.

He knew well enough that Selest

316

understood, with a clarity almost merciful, that this was the time of her life where stories diverged. In another life, she would walk away and remain clean. In this one, she would stay and become crucial.

Not good.

Not innocent.

Just decisive.

She was not just sacrificing her own life and the lives of others. She put her own integrity on that altar, knowingly. Maiser knew no one else capable of that. Not conscientiously. Not with their eyes open. Not while accepting pain that would never recede.

"Heartbeat normal," she said quietly, acknowledging him with the briefest turn of her head. "Vatslav, would you believe it? The third trimester ends in just a fortnight."

He nodded, not daring to voice the thought they both shared: they had made it this far, but this was still the easy part.

Little Rebekah in the cot sneezed and opened her eyes.

'Well, hello there!' said Maiser, leaning over her. 'Good morning, princess.'

The girl smiled and kicked her legs, knocking the neatly stretched blanket askew.

Selest turned to her. Maiser noticed the dark circles under her eyes, the way the lines around her mouth had deepened. She picked up the girl and said,

"She needs a bath and feeding. Vatslav, will you take her to the duty nurse? Please."

"You both need a bath and feeding. Forgive me, but you look weary, doctor. Why don't you let me finish your shift? Who's next?"

"Karagoz. She should be here in three quarters."

"If there's nothing to worry about, I'll wait for her and watch the monitors."

"Are you sure?"

"I'm sure. If nothing's happened all night, it's unlikely something will in the next forty-five minutes. By the way… this is what I came for. To give you this. It arrived with the night supplier."

Maiser lifted a hand holding a small package, wrapped in a plastic gift sheet decorated with green sparkles and flowers.

Selest sighed. 'Thank you. Leave it here. I'll open it later. You're right. I suppose I'm losing focus anyway, and you'll do a better job here.'

With Rebekah in her arms, she slowly left the chamber, and Maiser took the chair.

He checked the temperature fluctuations recorded through the night — eighteen distinct pulses, all curiously synchronised — and stifled a yawn. One tap on the control panel embedded in the desk, and the circular window behind him stirred to life. A single polished lens slid soundlessly aside and disappeared into the wall. Morning air poured in, crisp and cold. At this height — nearly seven hundred metres above the forest floor — the wind was clean, and for a moment you could almost believe the sky had remembered its original colour.

Why don't the loaders take the night shifts instead of the older woman? Or babysit for her? he thought when the first fifteen minutes passed. *They hardly need any sleep, have the stamina for more than eight hours of watch, and take fewer breaks. At the very least, they could've had enough compassion to come and replace her earlier.*

As if in answer, the door opened.

A young woman stepped in, strikingly beautiful. Her curly hair was a rare red that seemed to shift shade with the light, catching fire for a moment in the morning sun. Her eyes were dark brown, almost black, to match her name. Her plain clothes were of her own design, but well cut — she could have passed for a student from one of the Platinum Age's top academies. There was a faint, almost imperceptible hum from the micro-filaments in her sleeves as she moved.

"Morning, Mr Maiser," she said without a smile. "I heard the doctor didn't feel well enough to finish her shift. Thank you for covering her. You can go now."

It was said warmly enough, but with a thread of indifference — as if he'd been dismissed, told to remember his place. That was how it felt, anyway.

"You're welcome, miss," he replied with as much sarcasm as he could muster.

Karagoz stepped closer to the small table, her fingers brushing the shining parcel.

"What's this?" she asked.

"This was brought for Selest by midnight delivery, to be handed over at once. I was helping my technician fix the elevator, but thought I'd at least bring it here before she went off to rest."

He stopped, annoyed at himself. He didn't owe this girl an explanation. He wasn't a schoolboy, and she wasn't the headmistress. Why was she still touching it? Was she sensing something with her wired fingers?

"It's a bomb," Karagoz said, with the calmness of a statue. "Pre-programmed. And it's due to go off by 5:30 a.m."

Maiser looked at the clock on the screen.

5:29.

Thank you for finishing this book. The author would greatly appreciate an honest review if you're willing.

Thank you again.

ABOUT THE AUTHOR

Anka B. Troitsky, a multi-award-winning author and philosopher, came to the UK in 1993. With a rich background as a science teacher, translator of books, Law and NHS interpreter, she channels her diverse experiences and insights into the science fiction and fantasy genre, exploring the depths of what she has learned and understood throughout her journey.

You are welcome to Subscribe for an Email list:

www.ankatroitsky.com

Novels:
- ACT & VIST (- 1) short prequel
- OBJECT & VIST (1) 2021
- CONSTRUCT & VIST (2) 2022
- VIST & PROPER GANDA (3) 2023
- WHO WAS VIST (4) 2024

LitRPG Fantasy   LEVELLING UP TOGETHER. Series:
- THE FORGOTTEN FIVE.2025
- THE CURSE OF THE HALF-BREEDS 2026
- THE PRICE OF DOING RIGHT 2026